'You May Be Right, I May Be Crazy' and other stories

By Sreedevi Krishnan

This book is a collection of short stories published in various Indian magazines.

I Dedicate This Book

To

BANI GUHA THAKURTA, my closest friend, inspiration, author, a role model for all mothers and undoubtedly a beautiful human being with an enviable gift for giving.

Also by Sreedevi Krishnan

MUSINGS OF A SENSITIVE INDIAN WOMAN

SILICON CASTLES

ACKNOWLEDGEMENTS

A big 'Thank you' to Dr. Ahalya Krishnamoorthy, my scholarly, enthusiastic friend and exacting critic, who efficiently edited my manuscript and transformed it into a readable book.

This book would not have been possible without Cheenu and Jay, my two sons. I'm grateful for their encouragement, cheering presence and hours of assistance.

'Thanks' is an inadequate word to express my debt of gratitude to the endless list of my friends who not only willingly offered their shoulders to cry on during the darkest period of my life but also relentlessly persuaded me to resume my writing and move on.

PREFACE

It was not easy to offer a pattern for, 'You May Be Right, I May Be Crazy' and other stories. The stories are different in theme and length. Some are short, some are long. There are tragic stories and not so tragic stories. The themes too vary.

My title story deals with the practical wisdom of 'Forgiveness'.
The female protagonists in 'Return from the Ashes', 'Great Escape', 'Till Death Do Us part' reflect a wave of 'Feminism'.
While 'Chasing a Shadow' is about the ego and disastrous ambition of a Naval Officer, 'Key to the Gates of Heaven' is the pathetic end of a narcissistic woman.
'Dreams Shattered' is an attempt to portray 'feminization of poverty' through the exploitation of a poor, pretty innocent young girl.
'I Want to be like Kuttappan' is an innocent boy's deprived childhood to fulfill his ultra-modern, affluent, doctor parents' dream of making him a 'super brat'.
'Change of Heart' is about the sense of remorse in a young medical student while 'Truth of the Hereafter' deals with the only reality in anyone's life, 'death'.
'Silver Wedding Anniversary' and 'When Our Hitler Became a Hero' are autobiographical.
And the last story 'Happy Deevalley, I Love You Ma' ends in an optimistic note as love crosses all barriers of country, religion color or creed and makes a success of a marriage.

I agree that I focused on the lives of people around me as the basis of my stories. Naturally, numerous acquaintances and friends have in one way or the other found their way into the stories. This is done with the hope of providing authenticity to my stories. But the characters are fictitious and any resemblance to real people or experiences is purely coincidental. I sincerely hope my readers find the stories interesting.

Sreedevi Krishnan

Contents

'YOU MAY BE RIGHT, I MAY BE CRAZY'

Captain Shankar was watching the glassy sea through the porthole of his posh cabin. The deep blue sea and the millions of pinpoints cast by the blazing sun on it somehow dispelled all the gloomy thoughts from his mind. He experienced an inexplicable calm after a series of unfortunate incidents on board his ship in the past two weeks. Looking at the calm sea now, he could not believe that the sea had been extremely rough with a strong wind which strengthened to a gale only a couple of weeks ago. Though Captain Shankar never experienced sea-sickness, he hated the howling wind, the waves against the tossing ship, the creaking furniture, crashing bottles and shattering glasses around. Apart from the most unpleasant weather, the cranes of the ship too had failed. Once they were repaired, the cold storage went out of order resulting in a lot of wastage. The Chief Steward was in tears, when kilos of rotten mutton, vegetables and eggs were thrown into the sea. Once that was over, Chief Officer Suresh's two year old son developed rashes and high fever. Sailing with her son for the first time, Mrs. Suresh was panicky and inconsolable.

Finally, when the child recovered from his illness, the most unfortunate and unexpected thing happened, thirty -year old Radio Officer, Robins, died of a massive heart attack.......

Only a couple of weeks passed and it looked like an eternity. Even on a normal shore life, the death of someone, so young and healthy, like Robins was a great blow. But, on board the ship a death like that, affected everyone and took a very long time to recover from the shock. That was one thing about life on board the ship. They got so attached to each other and   a tragedy like that hit everyone so badly.

Captain remembered the radiant face of Robins, so full of life. He was not handsome; he was on the fat side. Despite his blunt nose, small beady eyes, and balding hair, he was charming. His sunny disposition, laughing mouth and readiness to help anyone in trouble endeared him to everyone. Being a voracious reader, he was such a help to captain in selecting good books, who loved to have a good collection for the ship's library. Robins was also in charge of exchanging videos with the other ships. Since he had a refined taste, the captain could absolutely rely on his Radio Officer for getting the choicest movies for the ship. His impeccable English and his alert nature took a load off the Captain's mind. In spite of being a tough task master and intolerant to slackness, Captain. Shankar had no complaints against Robins. In fact, he was full of praise for the Officer, who could joke and laugh heartily even in the midst of trouble.

"How could death snatch away such a lively person? He was just 30. If an experienced and detached person like me could be so much affected by Robin's death, how the Sureshs would feel his absence? Poor Mrs. Suresh broke down even when Robins was taken in the Neil Robertson stretcher to the hospital in Sydney. Thank God! I'm signing off in a day or two. I would certainly overcome all my traumatic experiences, the moment I reach my home. Six months with my loving family after this long separation would be real fun. No wonder they say, "Absence makes the heart grow fonder'. This time, I must buy Sherry the car I promised her when she got admission in the Medical College. Tomorrow I must go ashore and buy a swimming costume for her and some curios for Rohini, its sheer

fun to watch her face glowing with pride whenever I get some artifacts for her interior decoration. Cheenu wanted a pair of jeans, Oh, where did I keep his measurements? So forgetful after the tragic death of Robins. Again death—oh God, even when I try to think of something pleasant, Robins comes in between. Perhaps a drink may do some good," thought Captain Shankar.

Suddenly Captain's thoughts were interrupted by a loud knock on the door. "Yes, come in", said Captain, hardly concealing his irritation. But, when the Chief Officer came in, he was surprised. He was under the impression that the Chief Officer had gone ashore as he had already taken permission to go out with his wife, as she badly needed some diversion .Further, the moment she came to know about the ship's program, she had prepared a long list of things to buy from Hong Kong for their newly constructed house in his native place in Kerala.
"What happened? Why didn't you go out? Shopping in Hong Kong would have provided a good change for Mrs. Suresh, after all these tragic events. Your son Ranjit would've enjoyed the park here. There's a lovely park nearby".

The Chief Officer hesitated for a moment and then said in a hardly audible voice.
"Sir, can you spare some time for me? I've to discuss something very personal. If you think I'm disturbing you now, I'll come later."

Captain looked at him with scrutinizing eyes. He looked very weak; a week's stubble certainly did not suit his round face. His bushy eye brows, narrow, close set eyes, stubborn chin and the earlobes which reminded one of 'Buddha' made him look not only unapproachable, though funny, but also crafty and cunning. Somehow Captain was not fond of his Chief

Officer. He was arrogant, extremely selfish and lethargic to a great extent. Though Captain never spared him, it was always a strain to be civil to such a ruthless man. He tolerated him mainly because his wife was extremely good natured, and son, lovable. Being the only lady on board the ship, she endeared herself to everyone by her pleasant nature and culinary expertise. She enjoyed cooking some choicest dishes on every weekend and distributing to all the Officers and the crew. She must have been around thirty-five and was very ordinary-looking. She had unruly curly hair, which fell over her already narrow fore-head, blunt nose and thick lips. Though she looked plain and unattractive, everyone liked her because of her extremely good nature.

"No, no, I'm absolutely free now, c'mon, have a drink with me. I need a drink very badly to get rid of the unpleasant thoughts and it's a pleasure to have your company now, Suresh".

So saying, Captain quickly mixed two scotch-on-rocks and handed over a glass to the Chief Officer. While handing over the glass, Captain noticed that Suresh was not his usual self at all. He looked extremely frail and his hands almost trembled. He sank into the chair opposite to Captain. Captain tried hard to hide his puzzled expression and asked "What's the matter Suresh? Aren't you well?"

To Captain's surprise, the Chief Officer almost gulped down half a glass of whisky before he talked. As though gaining strength from the drink, he cleared his throat and said, "I'm okay, Sir, I mean, physically, but I'm so miserable and as I told you I've come to ask your advice on a purely personal matter. I wouldn't have ventured to discuss this problem, if I were to face you again. The fact that you're going away and perhaps

I won't set my eyes on you again, makes it easier for me to confide in you. Sir, it's about my wife, Nalini".

"Don't worry Suresh, you can trust me. I would never, ever betray the confidence you've in me".

Suresh began to speak in a low voice awkwardly as though he was ashamed and was desperate to get it off his chest. Suresh could not believe it was his own voice, it sounded like a stranger's voice, Why, even the bitter, agonizing experience was not his own, it happened to someone else. He was reduced to the status of a mere narrator, who could go through the tragic episode which shattered his entire life, matter of factly.

Suresh remembered the monotonous routine of a Chief Officer of a cargo ship. Rising before dawn, putting on the uniform, hurrying through the same breakfast of toast, eggs and fruit juice, carrying out the Captain's instructions, watching and supervising the loading and unloading of cargo, listening to the endless complaints of the crew and taking them to the captain etc. etc. .

Life on board was mechanical, boring and sometimes even maddening. A chief Officer under a stern, responsible Captain had no time for himself or his family during the hectic day. For that matter, everybody on board was busy except the Radio Officer, who could relatively relax. Naturally, the Chief Officer's wife Nalini and their three year old Ranjit were always with Robins. Robins was very fond of Ranjit, he was equally fond of the good food Nalini cooked frequently. Suresh remembered that, Robins and Nalini had so many things in common—good food, good movies, music and sight-seeing, Suresh could never sit through a movie, he had no ear for music either. When he had time he drank rather heavily and went to sleep. In fact, he was grateful to Robins for keeping company with his wife and son, when the ship sailed and for accompanying them on every port for sight-seeing and shopping. Nalini always had a long list of things to buy and enjoyed sight-seeing, clicking the camera on every beautiful spot. Suresh hated sight-seeing and had no patience to accompany Nalini on her endless shopping spree, carrying their son and answering his never-ending queries on all silly topics. So, he was very happy when Robins gladly took them around, whenever they reached a port. Even when Ranjit fell sick, Robins was a great help. Somehow, Robin's reassuring words always allayed Nalini's worst fears. Suresh found nothing unusual about Nalini's friendship or her enthusiasm to make special dishes for Robins, who affectionately called her, 'chechi', meaning 'elder sister' in Malayalam. Further, which mother would not like a man like Robins, who always amused, entertained and played with her unusually naughty, hyper active offspring?

Then, one day, soon after lunch, Robins collapsed. It was a panic-stricken Nalini, who rang up the Captain, who immediately called for the ambulance. In no time Robins was carried to the best hospital. In the evening, Nalini too went along with the Captain to visit Robins. The last conscious act of Robins was, to remove his gold chain with a crucifix and diamond ring and hand over to a sobbing Nalini.
That night, the Captain was shocked to receive the tragic news of Robins' death. It was impossible to believe that Robins, who was full of life was no more. Immediately after the Captain broke the news to Suresh, he rushed to his cabin. Ranjit was fast asleep and Nalini was on the rocking chair, lost in thought.

Suresh approached Nalini gently and said, "Nalini, I'm afraid, I've very bad news for you. *Hmmmm,* we just got the news that Robins passed away, ten minutes back. How terrible! I'm sure everyone on board the ship would be affected by his death. In any case we've to hide this from Ranjit because"……….. Before he could complete his sentence, Nalini gave a piercing cry and fell head long to the floor. She had fainted. Suresh lifted her up and laid her on the bed. He forced a little brandy between her parted lips. She slowly opened her eyes and cried "No, no, it's not true".

"Yes Nalini, it's true".

Nalini burst into tears. She wept convulsively. Suresh tried to touch her but she immediately withdrew her hands as though repelled and cried, "Please leave me alone, please leave me alone." It was really pathetic to see her body shaken by uncontrollable sobs. She was not herself. Suresh tried to hold her shoulders but he shook herself free –"For Heavens' sake, go away" She cried, "Oh, Danny, Danny, how could it happen? I just can't bear it; I just can't, my God, my God …."

Suresh was puzzled. He never heard her calling Robins 'Danny'. True, 'Daniel Robins' was his name but everyone on board called him 'Robins'. Suresh began to grow impatient. He could not believe that Nalini was capable of being so emotional. Nalini groaned as though in pain and tears streamed down from her staring eyes.

"C'mon Nalini, you would wake up Ranjit now. Remember, we shouldn't tell him about this. Try to pull yourself together. Here, have some more bandy, you would feel better, much better". Suddenly, Nalini sprang to her feet and pushed Suresh aside with all her strength. The glass of brandy fell from his hand, smashing the glass to smithereens. Suresh looked at his wife, puzzled. He could see that unmistakable hatred in her eyes.

"I wish I were dead too, please go away, Leave me alone, I beg you."

Suresh looked at Nalini's pathetic face, her staring eyes and her ringed neck adorned with Robins' chain and crucifix. All at once Suresh saw in her eyes something which shocked him. A shudder passed through his spine and hanging his head, he walked out of the cabin. He went to the saloon and drank to his heart's content. Then, he staggered to his cabin.

Nalini lay in the same position as he left her. Suresh sat on the chair, facing her.
"What was Robins to you, tell me, bitch", he thundered. Nalini wiped her tears with her palm and said, "It was a terrible shock, I wasn't myself". Her lips trembled.
"True, but how can you break down like this over Robins', just a friend's death? Hearing a friend's death, how can a strong woman like you faint straightaway or cry like this? And I never heard you calling him "Danny" before".

"How can you be so heartless? I was very fond of him, his death was so sudden, so unexpected that I could not bear it."
"Oh, c'mon Nalini, even your own brother's death was so sudden and so unexpected, but you didn't go pieces over it, you didn't display this much emotion. Then, you came to me for comfort, cried on my shoulder. Now, what happened? I want truth, nothing but truth. Don't take me for a fool."

Nalini looked at her drunken husband. She was too absorbed in her own grief to be concerned about him. She simply loathed his presence. Controlling her tears, she said, "Look, I'm very tired now, you're not very sober either. We'll talk tomorrow."

That was the last straw. Suresh held her wrist twisted it and screamed, "Speak now, bitch. I'll kill you, if you don't speak now, right now. Answer me, wasn't Robins your lover?"
Nalini hesitated a moment and then said in a very calm and clear voice, "Yes".

"Bitch", shouted Suresh. Holding Nalini's shoulder with his left hand, he slapped her cheeks with his strong right palm again and again till she sank to the floor............

Captain saw two tears welled up in his Chief Officer's eyes and slowly rolled down his cheeks. Captain could not help pitying the man in front of him. He quickly poured another stiff drink, which Suresh finished in a gulp. Replenishing his drink, Captain asked gently, "What're you planning to do Suresh?"

"I want your advice, Sir. I don't know what would happen to my son, if I divorce Nalini. She has no parents or anyone else to fall back upon. She's not even qualified to get a job and support herself."

"Divorce? Who asked you to divorce your wife? How could you even entertain such thoughts after living with her for more than a decade? She's your wife and mother of your smart, lovable son Ranjit."

"What do you mean Sir? She cheated on me. She's not even grateful. I've given her everything she wanted. You don't know her poverty-stricken existence before I married her. She fooled me all along. I transformed the shy, coy girl from a remote village in Kerala to a sophisticated, refined lady. What would happen to my honor, if I continue to live with a woman like that?"
Captain laughed, one of his rare, light-hearted laugh and said, "C'mon Suresh, don't try to cut off your nose to spite your face. You said, she's so ungrateful. But, tell me, why did you take so much pains to reform that village girl? Well, it's to boost your own ego, Suresh. Moreover you say, you gave her everything she wanted, everything which your money could buy. But, are you sure that you gave her everything she needed, secretly craved for? I've lived in this planet for many more

years than you've done and I tell you, there's a lot of difference between a woman's "needs" and "wants". Women need love and tender care. You can't take them for granted".

Suresh could not believe his ears. He frowned. What about his self-respect, sense of decency? He never expected the Captain to be so logical, so unsympathetic, so unfeeling.

"You've no idea, Sir, how this hurts me. How can you be so unsympathetic? How can I continue to be the husband of a woman, who loved another man? I feel terrible."

"Suresh, I understand your feelings. But I feel strongly that, the only way you could hurt your wife back, is by forgiving her. Your generosity alone will bring out that sense of remorse in her. And believe me, she would love you with all her heart and serve you throughout her life with such fierce loyalty that no husband could ever dream of. Besides, Robins is dead and you can't possibly be jealous of a dead man. No one knows about this love affair except your wife, you and now, me. I'll be signing off tomorrow. So, let bygones be bygones. I know Nalini; she's a warm, kind-hearted and lovable person. Listen to me Suresh, my voice of experience. What's love after all? I loved and married, after thirty years of married life, I can tell you that love's only a physical attraction, the border line between love and infatuation is very thin. The so called love is often generated by propinquity, like in your wife's case. I know it's hard, but try and forgive your wife. Remember, she needs you more than ever in her life to get over Robins' sudden death and her passing fancy towards him. If you forgive her now, trust me Suresh, she would love you, respect you, till her dying day.

Suresh was almost convinced by the Captain's arguments. Perhaps it was his fault too that he took Nalini so much for granted. Captain was right; he was not sure whether he gave her everything she needed.

"I was not a loving, caring husband to Nalini, brought up in an extremely traditional 'Nair' family, I made the mistake of thinking that women are inferior to men and therefore need not be respected. I always bossed over her, how many times I had hurt her feelings deeply, comparing her to pretty, accomplished wives of my friends. Did I ever appreciate her efforts in frequenting beauty parlors, wearing mod attires and trying to sport a sophisticated look of the women I compared her with? I never left a single chance of bringing up her middle-class background, calling it "poverty-stricken existence'. I never, not even once, complimented her on her culinary expertise or talent in music and dance. Isn't it natural for her to fall for Robins, who, not only admired her for all her achievements but also loved and cared for her son. As captain said, women need tender loving care. Further forgiving Nalini is the most practical solution to the problem. My forgiveness would certainly torture her conscience and she would do everything possible to make amends. Now that I realize my mistake, I'll treat her with love and affection. Actually I can use this unfortunate episode to strengthen our bond instead of destroying our marriage."

Suresh smiled for the first time after a miserable, torturing week.

"Thank you Sir, thank you very much for your advice. Oh, a heavy load off my mind now and I feel extremely relieved after listening to you, oh yes, your voice of experience. Sir, I'll be grateful to you forever. God bless you, Sir; have a great time with your family." Suresh got up, shook hands with the captain and hurriedly descended the staircase towards his cabin, with determined steps. He could not help smiling, when he heard the voice of Billy Joel from the saloon, "You may be right, I may be crazy…"

WHEN OUR 'HITLER' BECAME A HERO

"We'll call him Ginger", said my daughter enthusiastically.

"No, we'll call him 'Whisky'", suggested my husband, apparently keeping in mind the true tradition of the Navy.

A thunderous 'No' from my son shook the entire house.

"He is somebody to be feared, a great force to reckon with. After all, he is a German, Doberman Pinscher, what do you say, mom?"

I looked at my happy family, seated in a circle around the wailing brown pup and admiring that shapeless thing with flopping ears and a tongue that lolled out like a lump of dark red wool, a one-inch stump in the place of a tail (I'm told that a Doberman's tail is cut off as soon as it is born) I certainly could not share their enthusiasm.

To begin with, let me confess that I'm not an animal lover. In fact my husband has been trying unsuccessfully for the past ten years to impress upon me the necessity of bringing up a watch-dog. First he said very poetically that the greatest urge of any human being was to love and to be loved. "Don't we need an emotional 'anchor' (again the 'Ship' language?) Who could fill up the gap better than a pet dog? Don't you agree with me that a dog could be much more faithful and grateful than our own children?"

When I refused to be convinced, he started another line of argument. "Look, I'm away from home, most of the time, considering the thefts, house-breakings and murders around, don't we ne need some sort of safety, protection from criminals?"

Children too joined my husband and soon I was fighting a lone battle against the idea of buying a dog. Finally I had to give in, when I heard how a pretty, petite Rajalakshmi hoodwinked my smart, clever, worldly-wise neighbor, Prema Nagarajan, and walked away with jewelry weighing twenty five sovereigns.

As the story goes, a charming confidence-trickster Rajalakshmi went inside Mrs. Nagarajan's flat about 11 in the morning, pretending to be her daughter Rama's friend. She enquired after her engagement to a green-card holder, engineer in Los Angeles. Mrs. Nagarajan was most eloquent, as usual about her great luck in getting an NRI son-in-law and narrated everything in minutest detail, right from the bride-seeing to the engagement. Rajalakshmi listened to her patiently, then went inside their bedroom on the pretext of tying her sari and flicked off the jewelry from the cupboard and walked away, that too, after drinking the steaming hot coffee offered by the gleaming Mrs. Nagarajan.

Would this have happened, if she had kept a watch-dog?

Well, I was thoroughly convinced and the next few days, all of us frantically went through the "Kennels and pets" columns of our newspaper. Finally, my husband and daughter went, and bought a 15 days' old Doberman pup, paying a formidable sum of Rs. 5000, which came as a rude shock to me…..

"C'mon ma, Isn't 'Hitler' a suitable name for him?" insisted my son.

"Leave me out of this naming ceremony for God's sake. Paying Rs. 5000 for this wailing pup was ridiculous. You must've been cheated .To think that we've to spend another Rs 1000 every month for his milk, eggs , meat and vitamins , call him 'white elephant', that would be more appropriate", I could not conceal my disapproval.

"What do you know? The choicest and most ferocious blood is running in this pup's veins, father, champion, KCI registered, thank our stars that we got it so cheap considering the demand for pedigreed pups now", waving the pedigree sheet in front of me, my husband thundered.

"Ignore her, Appa, she's always a wet blanket," that was my daughter.

"Let's take a decision about his name, I tell you 'Hitler' suits him, said my son emphatically and a chorus of 'Hitler' went up to the skies. Despite the clapping and deafening chorus, 'Hitler' continued his wailing non-stop that day.

Slowly Hitler got adjusted to the new surroundings, in about six months he grew up into a ferocious–looking but handsome dog. He was unusually tall and had a shining, velvety brown coat, shapely head with hazel eyes, long snout and flopping ears. He ran around the compound breaking all my favorite potted plants. But I stoically bore the loss, hoping that Hitler was going to be feared and respected by everyone. But alas that was not to be!

Hitler, no doubt, had a large frame and forbidding appearance on the whole. But that was all. He developed such a love for 'humanity' which would have made Adolf Hitler hang his head in shame. The moment our gate is clicked, Hitler would become alert, stand up looking towards the gate anxiously. By the time anyone entered the gate, he went blindly charging forward. Then, he stood before the intruder, wagging his one-inch stump relentlessly, body curved up, waiting to be patted. When patted or stroked, he would melt immediately, roll his hazel eyes, and wag his tail more vigorously as if to say, "I'm really sorry that I frightened you, I was only trying to welcome you."

Our Hitler certainly was a symbol of universal love and brotherhood. He did not confine his love to humanity alone. He loved crows, sparrows, mice, chameleons and even befriended cats and shared his food with all of them. But, strangely he developed an inexplicable hatred towards squirrels.

Squirrels seemed to be his born enemies. When squirrels scampered up and down the clump of trees, he barked at them continuously. If they happened to come down, he chased them around; he even caught a squirrel and killed it, in spite of our desperate attempts to save the innocent victim. His hatred towards squirrels was quite puzzling to everyone except my daughter, who acted as the Devil's advocate and said firmly, "Just like Hitler hated Jews and sent them to gas chambers mercilessly, our Hitler too hates squirrels, in any case squirrels are real nuisance, they chew up all our coconut flowers and eat up all our mangoes and guavas before they are ripened."

"As though his enmity towards squirrels is of any use to me. All my jasmine flowers, banana leaves and even tender coconuts are stolen regularly, right under his nose. What does he do the whole day except eating and sleeping? Someone regularly climbs the wall and plucks all these things, when we're away and he doesn't do a thing about it. What a disgrace!!"

"Hitler doesn't sleep a wink at night. I've seen him going around the house and watching it all night. In fact, his presence gives me courage to study late at night, when you're all fast asleep. Anyway, why should he worry about petty thefts? If there's a serious crime, I mean a major theft, I'm sure he would prove his true mettle," my daughter defended Hitler vehemently.

But I kept on grumbling that Hitler was only a nuisance as far as I'm concerned. Apart from the considerable expenditure on his daily meat, eggs and milk, I had to take him to the Veterinary Hospital for his periodical checkup, vitamin injections and regular immunizations. When Hitler was two, as suggested by his Vet, we gave an advertisement in 'The Hindu' for mating him. I was overjoyed as each 'successful mating' would entitle the male dog's owner, the option of either claiming the best pup or the price of it (*Huh!* how nice to know that even among canines, 'dowry 'is acceptable!)

The very next day of our advertisement, a black Doberman bitch was brought to our house in an air-conditioned, chauffeur-driven car. A jean-clad, charming, English lady, obviously the proud owner of the bitch also accompanied her. 'Diana', our Hitler's bride, was brought to our verandah. Hitler, ignoring Diana completely, went to her owner, curved up his body, and wagged his tail and waited anxiously to be stroked on his head. The moment the lady stroked him, he shook hands with her, licked her and wagged his tail relentlessly, as if to say that he is extremely honored by her very presence.
"Oh! He's very friendly, a real Hitler to look at, he has already fallen for my princess", so saying the lady gently pushed her Diana in front of Hitler. That was all; Hitler snarled at Diana, pounced on her and nearly bit her ears. Diana's loud wailing coupled with our combined screams for 'help', brought my son, who heroically controlled Hitler with all his strength and Diana with her owner took to their heels, without even bothering to look back.

Despite the nightmarish experiences, my hope too triumphed over experience and I tried my luck once more. But, a similar feat was repeated in the case of another bitch too, proving Hitler's hatred towards the bitches. *Huh!* Another striking similarity with Adolf Hitler, *'Hail Hitler'*.

Hitler continued his uneventful, all the same, enjoyable life, by eating, sleeping, welcoming strangers, playing with crows, chameleons, cats and mice, but of course, chasing and barking at squirrels. Over the years, I learnt not only to tolerate Hitler but also to love him for what he was. After all, when I come tired after a day's work, he was the only one to welcome me by galloping towards the gate, vigorously wagging his tail and licking me, to show how much he missed me.

Hitler kept company with me, when my husband sailed off and children stayed away in hostels. As time passed, he understood every syllable we uttered, shared our joys and sorrows. When my husband came home after a spell of separation, he welcomed him, licking him all over and circling around him, without letting him move away, his hazel eyes conveying the message, "Don't you see how I missed you, missed you so much ,much more than you could ever imagine?"

If a suitcase was packed for any member of the family to leave, Hitler at once sensed it and bid 'goodbye', shedding tears .He became the most lovable member of the family and we celebrated his birthday in May, by giving him presents and taking him to beach for playing in the water. Even I, who was once Hitler's worst critic, started loving him from the bottom of my heart.

Then, one night the most unexpected incident happened---Our Hitler rose to the rank of a great hero. Yes, he was instrumental in nabbing a notorious criminal gang involved in a series of crimes and murders for gain, not only in Chennai but also in Karnataka and Kerala.

One night our Hitler's deafening barks near the compound wall separating our house from the National bank, woke up not only us but also the entire neighborhood. In no time, people came running from all directions with flashing torch lights, to find a few masked men working on the strong, grilled entrance of the bank.

Resisting all attempts to go near them by pelting stones and throwing knives, they ran. Meanwhile, the armed Police alerted by a phone call arrived at the scene and after a hot chase, caught the gang. During the robbers' stoning operation, a stone hit Hitler on his forehead and he was bleeding. My daughter immediately attended to him, sutured and bandaged his wound.

Imagine my surprise when I got a call from the Police Commissioner next morning, thanking me profusely for the wonderful performance of Hitler, without which, they would never have caught this notorious criminal gang!

Hitler became a hero overnight. Newspapers carried an impressive account of his heroism under his photo with his bandaged forehead. Our relatives, friends, neighbors and even strangers sang *'hosannas' to* Hitler.

After a couple of days, in a glittering function, before the flashing of TV cameras, Inspector General of Police garlanded the 'hero' and presented him with a cheque of Rs.2000 and a medal. An advertising company advanced Rs.1000 and booked him for an advertisement. Though unaware of the historical significance of his non-stop barking on that fateful night, Hitler enjoyed the publicity and looked every bit a hero.

But, the very next day of this attempted robbery, I carefully surveyed the other side of my compound wall and amused to see a brown nest with two baby squirrels swishing their bushy tails, which had obviously fallen from our mango tree. At last, the mystery of Hitler's heroism was solved. But, my children argued vehemently, that the way Hitler barked as he had done never before, proved clearly that he had barked at the criminals, who tried to break open the grilled entrance to the bank. I only wondered, what Hitler would have done, if he had the powers of speech, would he have confessed the real cause of his unusually loud bark and shattered the pedestal under his feet or enjoyed the greatness thrust on him?!!

RETURN FROM THE ASHES

Lissy's hurried walk turned into a desperate run, when she saw the yellow-striped, over-crowded bus was about to start. But, with confidence induced by her twenty years' of bus-travel, she managed to push through the young, adventurous footboard travelers, boarded the bus and sank into the window seat. After getting a ticket to the 'New Looks' stop, Lissy leaned back comfortably in her seat, glanced at her watch showing 7.30 and heaved a sigh of relief. She was on time for her appointment at 9 in the beauty parlor.

Lissy could not help smiling, when she remembered the stern warning by Sheila, "Lissy, you must be there by 9, just when Mrs. Mehta starts her parlor. You're her first client, and she's very busy. With much difficulty, I registered your name, and I won't forgive you if you mess it up by going late. You know, I would've come with you but for the PTA meeting in Roshini's School. And Shamna too, is away, Anyway, don't worry, all the best," Sheila said and squeezed her palm.

When Lissy thought of her young friends Sheila and her cousin Shamna, tears welled in her eyes; how her life had changed from a living hell to something worth-living.
"Flower shop, Flower shop," the conductor's screaming and a shrill whistle, brought Lissy back to the present. She sighed deeply, sat on the edge of the seat and looked through the window. The huge flower shop with artistically arranged bouquets, neatly arranged red roses, marigolds, deep orange December-flowers, heaps and heaps of jasmine buds irritated her. The jasmines,

although looked splendid, infuriated her. Lissy closed her eyes tight. Though she could almost get over her phobia for jasmine, yes, she did not dread at its sight anymore - she could not help the revulsion they generated.   Jasmine garlands reminded her of her marriage to Rajan - a marriage that had gone wrong from day one, his addiction to alcohol, his crude abusive sex, his violence followed by his tears of repentance, promises and pleadings not to leave him and several unpleasant memories.

Somehow, those deliberately-forgotten years enveloped Lissy again, and her mind raced back to the day Rajan and his parents visited her house for the official 'bride-viewing'. Amma, proud of Lissy's curly, lustrous hair, braided it and adorned it with lots of jasmine buds and insisted on Lissy wearing her light blue georgette sari with pearl accessories. Lissy remembered her Amma's angry retort, when Asok, her elder brother made fun of her dark complexion in spite of Amma's home-made 'fairness cream'- made of turmeric, rose water and cream of milk, which she applied daily.

"Oh shut up Asok, can't you see how charming my daughter is? Though dark, she has a flawless complexion, sparkling eyes and a lovely smile like Vidya Balan.   That boy is lucky, my daughter is a Virgo; she would bring him luck. Just you wait and see."

'Poor Amma, if only she were alive! She was too young to die, just in her early fifties, that too barely after a couple of months after my marriage. Oh! She was a tower of strength, and I could've leaned on her forever. She certainly would not have been like my father, who was complacent about performing his fatherly duties by marrying me off to one of the richest families of Nagerkoil, that too, as he used to say, "Giving a fat

*dowry and lots of jewelry to compensate for Lissy's
dark complexion, a legacy from her mother's side."*

*Asok whom I admired so much, turned out to be the
worst opportunist. Our mother's unexpected death and
my broken marriage took him closer to his goal of
being a Doctor in the USA. Now, well-settled in the
USA, his responsibility to our octogenarian father is
limited to the fixed amount sent to an Old Age Home in
Kerala, for father's stay.*

*Looking back, I think, Amma had some premonition
about the impending disaster. How she had insisted on
my continuing with my job even after the
marriage! Come to think of it, it was her childhood
friend, Miss. John, the then Principal, who had
appointed me in this very school, years ago, twenty
years ago. How time flew!*

*Perhaps it was my Amma's blessings that at least I
could retain my sanity and hold on to my job as a
teacher, despite the physical and mental torture I had to
endure from Rajan, my violent, alcoholic husband. "A
humanly impossible feat," as Shamna often remarked.'*

"New-looks stop, New-looks stop," the conductor
screamed, and Lissy got up from her seat, pushed
through the crowd, got out of the bus and walked
towards the beauty parlor in rapid strides. With an
impressive banner of a semi-nude, beautiful girl with an
hour-glass figure, holding a bouquet of roses, the parlor
seemed attractive.

Lissy looked around to make sure that none of the
passersby was watching her entering the famous beauty
parlor. *'Won't they be amused to see a dark, ordinary
looking woman in her fifties, visiting the beauty
parlor?'*

*'Oh, c'mon, why should I be bothered about other
people's opinion - that too after so many years of
divorce? Am I still haunted by Rajan's most insulting*

words of my being dark, ugly and unsophisticated? It's time I get rid of my complex and move on. Perhaps Sheila's right, this National award for the Best Teacher, this recognition of my work, and love and respect of my innumerable students must prove as a turning point in my life too', she thought.

Once inside, the air conditioned room with swivel chairs, recliners, mirrors, marble countertops cluttered with attractive, colorful containers with creams, lotions, combs and brushes of various sizes and colors and other unfamiliar objects made Lissy nervous. Besides, she could feel four pairs of scrutinizing eyes of very young girls, uniformly dressed in white blouse, green and white checkered short- skirts which stopped well above their knees and matching olive green aprons. Trying hard to conceal her nervousness, Lissy cleared her throat and asked for Mrs. Mehta.
"Please sit down, madam," said the tallest of the girls with slanting eyes and well-arched eyebrows. "Mrs. Mehta's expecting you," she added and went inside.

In no time, a tall, fair, slim lady with an equine face in blue jeans and red *Kurtis* appeared. Giving her best smile, she said very politely, "I'm Madhu, Madhu Mehta, you're Lissy, right? Your friends Sheila and Shamna are my regular clients." Then, turning towards the tall girl, she ordered, "hair dye, bleaching and facial, manicure, pedicure and body massage; get all the imported items, quick." Lissy could hear her heart-beats as she brought only Rs. 1000 to pay for her beauty treatment and a shawl for her Delhi trip. Would that be enough?

As though answering Lissy's unasked question, Mrs. Mehta raised her jet black, well-shaped eye-brows, which, gave her a perpetual 'surprised' look, and said, "It's all paid for, it's your friends' treat for your getting National award for the Best Teacher; by the way, my hearty congrats, we're lucky, it's not every day we could be of service to celebrities."

Though puzzled by Sheila and Shamna's unexpected, generous gesture, Lissy was amused to hear her being referred to as a 'celebrity'. She could almost hear Rajan's sneering remarks after a few drinks, a prelude to his usual violence, "who would've married you except a fool like me? Short, dark and rustic, worse than our maid. Except for your convent English, you'd have been mistaken for my servant. Thank God, that old woman, your mother, had the sense to send you to a good School and Training College; at least you've a definite income, although a pittance, from the school."

Lissy, returning to the present, smiled and said, "Thanks, but I'm a very ordinary teacher, and, honestly, I'm surprised I'm chosen for an honor like this,"
Handing Lissy a loose, front open gown to put over her sari, Mrs. Mehta said, "Oh, that's very modest of you; your friends think the world of you. Looks like, the first time you're inside a beauty parlor, don't worry, just relax, I'm sure, you would enjoy our attention and would visit us regularly with your friends."

Once Mrs. Mehta left the place, two girls came forward. One of them removed Lissy's hair -do and exclaimed, "Wow, what lustrous hair, you don't have much gray either." Then with an amazing dexterity she parted Lissy's curly hair with the long handle of the comb, combed and clipped it while the other girl applied hair dye with a smooth brush, taking care to wipe off drops of dye from her forehead.

Choking with unshed tears, Lissy remembered her Amma massaging medicated oil on her thick, curly hair and insisting her washing it off after about an hour, with homemade hibiscus leaves' shampoo, an unfailingly regular ritual, every Sunday.

Lissy inhaled deeply, remembering her Amma's uncontrollable crying and sobbing, when she left for Chennai, after her marriage.

'Although I too shed token tears, I was full of excitement, love and pride for the well-built, handsome husband; perhaps, my head was clouded with romantic, private dreams which I've woven with the help of all those romantic novels and poems. What is more, I knew I could cook very well and find my way to Rajan's heart through his stomach. And if love could win him over, who would be a better wife than me, with all the love and compassion drilled into my head from early childhood? I was almost sure of my looks as my Amma and my friends kept praising my charm despite the dusky complexion. Ah!! What a jolt it was to my overconfidence on my very first night?'

"Oh, ma'am, you dozed off? I'll apply this natural color nail polish which would suit you", the girl attending to her feet gently shook her shoulder. Lissy could not help admiring the good job done by the two girls, who managed to work simultaneously and finished hair-dyeing, manicure and pedicure, in less than an hour.

"Now, close your eyes ma'am for shaping your eyebrows and upper lip. After this, Mrs. Mehta will do your facial in the next room," said the ever smiling girl, pointing towards the bigger room. Once they started moving the thread back and forth on her eyebrows, tears flowed from Lissy's closed eyes.

"Hurting? Because this is the first time, sorry, sorry, it's over", said one of the girls.

'Hurting? Huh! Poor girl, what did she know about the pain I had endured for five long years?'

"Please go and lie down on the cot in the next room, for your facial."

The girl's words brought Lissy back to the present.
The dimly lit, spacious air- conditioned room, cozy bed and the melodious Hindi film-song flowing from the stereo, strangely reminded Lissy of her first night in the five star Hotel-suite, where they had their wedding reception.

Lissy waited in all her bridal finery for Rajan to come and admire her. After all, she knew she looked charming in deep blue sari with intricate *zari* design with a matching Safire and pearl studded necklace, ear drops and a bracelet - her Amma's special gift and an elaborate hair-do with pearls and jasmine buds pinned on it, highlighting her slender neck and glowing face. Not only her Amma, her constant confidence-booster, but also her colleagues showed surprise at her metamorphosis. *"You look so much like Nanditha Das now,"* they chorused.

Lissy knew Rajan was too busy shaking hands with innumerable guests even to notice, leave alone comment on her looks. So, she waited for Rajan to come and see her in all her bridal ensemble.

Suddenly, Rajan pushed the door open and exclaimed, "My God! Still wearing your bridal outfit, for Heavens' sake, change into something comfortable. Looking at you, I'm getting suffocated," he laughed, his loud, contemptuous laugh, curling his lips upwards.

Once inside the bathroom, controlling her unshed tears, Lissy tried to justify Rajan. 'How silly of me, behaving like a moon-struck teenager when, I'm on the wrong side of twenty and a respectable school teacher and a role model for young girls? Further, how can I expect Rajan, a successful, middle aged business man to behave like a road side Romeo?"

Lissy hurried back to the room in her imported negligee- her aunt's gift, toweling her wet, lustrous hair vigorously. Rajan was busy switching off the bright lights and putting on soft music. Without even lifting his head, he said, "Lie down and take some rest, I'll join you after a few seconds."

Lissy lay down, and the soft bed, dimly lit room with the romantic film song flowing from the music system, made her doze off. Suddenly, she was woken up by the gurgle slurp of Rajan's drinking. Through half-opened eyes, she saw her husband sitting on the edge of the bed and drinking from an exquisitely designed glass. Lifting his drink, he said, "Cheers, this is whisky on the rocks, I need at least two pegs a day, Doctor's orders, you see, best for de-stressing; want to try? This is not the cheap stuff your Nagarcoil men drink," he laughed, his villainous laugh. Before Lissy could react, he added, 'don't sleep off darling, our first night is not meant to be wasted on it.

The rest was a nightmare. As Lissy was dozing off, she felt the weight of Rajan on her. Soon she felt his rough, frenzied fingers squeezing her nipples, and exploring the various parts of her body. She felt a sharp pain when he moved deeper and deeper into her. Before she could get over the shock and react to his assault, she heard her husband's exulting, repulsive grunts, which muffled her cries of utter despair and helplessness.

Nauseated, she dragged herself to the bathroom for a hot shower, to clean her filthy body of alcohol and tobacco stench. By the time Lissy was back in the bedroom, she found her husband snoring.

From then on, she dreaded sex. She could not believe what had happened to her that night, that hurtful, humiliating act instead of the pleasant surprise she had been waiting for was sex.

Days and weeks crawled by. Lissy realized with a shock that, Rajan was a compulsive alcoholic and his rich parents forced him into marriage, hoping it would reform him. Once Lissy left for school, Rajan returned home to drink and drown his 'business worries'. And Lissy became the punching bag for all his failures. He often would say, "Your people cheated me. What are rupees Ten lakhs and some junk jewelry as a dowry for a dark girl like you? You're not even capable of giving birth to my child. Your aunt, your father's sister has no children, and this runs in the family. I wouldn't have touched drinks if I were blessed with a child."

As time progressed, Rajan stopped going to his so-called office and stayed at home. Lissy had to get up early, prepare a whole meal for him before starting for her school, all the time tolerating his filthy remarks. "You're a flirt, the way you dress up for the school, as though you're going for your first date. What's the point in your make up, black like coal? *Thooo!*"

Lissy dreaded nights; tired and exhausted after a day's hard work, when all Lissy wanted was sleep Rajan would invariably approach her to satisfy his lust. Lissy experienced the truth behind the Bard's words, "Alcohol provokes the desire but takes away the performance."

If she refused sex, he became violent, "You're a flirt, as though I don't know how you lived in your hostel, away from home, happily going around with men."

Even after so many years, Lissy shuddered at the thought of Rajan's face, his bloodshot eyes flashing fire, his flared up nostrils and lips curling upwards while he twisted his leather belt on his fist. Panting like an animal, with gritted teeth, he beat her black and blue with the belt and then slept off peacefully. The next morning, he would come with jasmine flowers, packed breakfast, and medicines. Adorning her hair with flowers, he would force her to eat. Then, with tears in his eyes, he would apply medicine on her cuts and bruises, apologize profusely for his violence and promise never to repeat his inhuman behavior. But, his promises were like *pappads* meant to be broken invariably after a couple of days.

Slowly the wife in Lissy had died but the teacher in her stayed strong because of her indomitable will to survive. She concentrated more on her job, took extra care to groom her students for cultural activities which provided an outlet for her talents: love for music, theatre and oratorical skills. When Lissy's students not only bagged most of the prizes in Inter-School competitions, but also won top ranks in the Board Exam, the School management recognized Lissy's efforts and promoted her as the Head of the Dept. of English.

One night, when Lissy resisted Rajan's sexual assaults, he shook her shoulders violently and yelled, "I understand your aversion to sex; you've fun with all those grown up boys, supposed to be your students, s-t-u-d-e-n-t-s, and yes ... The question is what are you teaching them in the name of extra, e-x-t-r-a activities?"

That was the limit. Clenching her teeth, Lissy said, "What a sick mind you've, you need psycho..." Before she could complete her sentence, Rajan held her by her long hair, dragged her to the bathroom, and slammed her face into the wall repeatedly.

Lissy's two weeks' medical leave and dentures on the front row of teeth were, as before, explained away as the result of her temporary black out and hitting against the stone wall of the bathroom. Her colleagues, except for the bubbly Sheila, believed her explanation or at least pretended to be satisfied. Sheila, being the Music and Dance teacher, worked closely with Lissy for training students for the Inter-School cultural meets. In the course of time, they became close friends, but Lissy could not confide in Sheila, her marital problems and spoil her happiness. Sheila, however, noticed the permanent sadness in Lissy's eyes and could not understand. Lissy's reluctance to talk about Rajan. Although she didn't buy Lissy's usual excuse of 'slipping and falling' whenever there was a visible injury, she never bothered Lissy for details, for fear of losing her friendship. Even when she wanted to visit Lissy during Lissy's medical leave, she found Lissy's excuse that Rajan did not like to entertain visitors as lame. Later, Lissy's explanation of her black out, falling and losing her two front teeth, was too hard to believe, and she confided in Shamna, her advocate cousin, her worst fears about Lissy's life.

That eventful Saturday, Lissy was relaxed as Rajan had left for Coimbatore on work. Clad in a new blue Bengal cotton sari and blouse and looking presentable, Lissy reached the School, with a big parcel of mutton cutlets for Sheila, who always appreciated Lissy's cooking.

At lunch interval, just when Sheila was trying to convince Lissy to go with her to her place, Sheila's cell phone rang and it was Shamna, her cousin pleading with her to meet her at 'Satyam' theater, as she had three tickets for the matinee show of the much talked about film "Provoked."

Sheila was all enthusiasm, "Yes I'm coming with Lissy, and don't dispose of the extra ticket. Lissy brought lots of cutlets too; we'll be there in half an hour."

Then she pleaded with Lissy, "*C'mon* Lissy, be a sport, you'll be home by 5.30. You can see Nandita Das, your look-alike, please, please, please, it's great movie with Aishwarya Rai as heroine."

It was ages since Lissy watched a movie in peace, leave alone go to a theater. With Rajan away in Coimbatore, that was the ideal day. What's more she could meet Shamna, the smart, advocate cousin of Sheila.

Lissy was excited like a teenager. She experienced a tremendous sense of freedom, a great relief from the usual tension and fear. But, her happiness and excitement gave way to a deep sense of sadness and depression, when the married life of the heroine, the unfortunate victim of physical and emotional abuse was unraveled. It was not Aishwarya Rai anymore; it was Lissy and her life with Rajan, on the screen.

Lissy tried to control her tears; she did not want to upset her good friends. But, she did not know when, why or how, a violent sob escaped her and how they all reached the Working Women's Hostel, where Shamna lived.

After an hours' of uninterrupted crying and sobbing, Lissy regained her calm and she heard herself narrating everything, every single detail of her married life, unashamedly, to the shell shocked Shamna and Sheila.

Wiping their tears and hugging Lissy close, both Sheila and Shamna asked in unison, "How could you, an educated, talented and charming person, put up with that beast? It's unbelievable!"

"No. Lissy, you're not going back to that beast, I can't let you go," said Sheila, her face showing shock, pain, terror and anxiety.

"Lissy, this way, you're going to end up either in suicide or murder, No, no, you're not going back, you're going to stay here, right here, in this hostel from tonight. I can fight the divorce case for you free of cost, but I won't let you go." It was Shamna with an unmistakable ring of authority in her voice.

"Yes, Lissy, don't go, I wish you had confided in me earlier, I never bought your stories of slipping and falling or the latest black out. You should've run away from him long ago," said Sheila.
Hah! What did they know how much a woman could tolerate, when she was scared, when she had   no place to escape, or none to fall back upon?

Everything else happened in lightning speed. As Lissy did not claim any alimony or even her dowry back, 'divorce by mutual consent' was granted.

"Now, look, how pretty you're with this light make up after our facial," Mrs. Mehta said and thrust a hand mirror on Lissy. Lissy could not recognize her own reflection; she looked years younger, with the dyed hair, shaped eyebrows, glowing complexion and a touch of makeup. "Thank you, thank you so much," she beamed.

While walking towards the auto- rickshaw stand, Lissy thought, '*My mother would've been certainly proud to watch me rise from the ashes like the proverbial phoenix; perhaps she's already watching me from above*'. A cool breeze through the road-side trees caressed Lissy like her beloved Amma and filled her with great hope and confidence for a new beginning, a new life.

GREAT ESCAPE

Seated on a rickety chair in a narrow cubicle of a Working women's Hostel, Rajalakshmi started her first long letter to her parents, after her marriage two years ago. She was perfectly calm and felt a sense of immense relief after filing her divorce petition. But, she wondered how her poor, old parents would react to her decision. After all, hadn't they sunk their entire life-savings to buy her a husband? Besides, wasn't she brought up to believe in the sanctity of marriage and the sacred duty of a wife to serve her husband however worthless he was? And won't they be ostracized by the Orthodox Brahmin community for her unpardonable crime? A series of confusing and uncomfortable thoughts flashed across her mind. But, somehow she was in no mood to worry about her parents or the Society's disapproval. She had suffered enough, like the proverbial phoenix she raised herself from the tragedy and started picking up the lost thread of life. She did not want any force on earth to disturb her calm now. With firm determination, she began writing the letter narrating her bitter, agonizing experiences with no tears, no sobs, in fact with no emotion as though she was writing about someone else's experiences. But, while her fingers moved on, she could not help her mind racing back thereby opening the flood gate of memories......

Rajam remembered that she had no looks to her credit. She was a very ordinary looking, dark-complexioned girl. But, her husband and in -laws should be grateful to her looks and dark skin.

'My looks and complexion certainly strengthened their bargaining power; otherwise who would have paid Rs 3 lakhs in cash, jewelry, and a lavish wedding in a posh marriage hall for just a lecturer in a private College and the only bread-winner in his family? After all that, the humiliation, suffering and starvation till I decided to run away. How I hate them all, that woman Lakshmi, my mother-in-law, her spineless husband, her cruel son Sudarsan who, tied the 'thaali' around my neck and took the seven steps amidst the chanting of mantras' and yet was a silent spectator to all the tortures and humiliation I was subjected to. Wasn't his mother a hardened criminal and he, her accomplice? Both mother and son must be happy to receive my Divorce notice. Once the divorce comes through he could get married to another innocent girl who might bring even more dowry. After all divorce is not a stigma for as a man is concerned. What strange double standards! A widower can get married barely a couple of months after his wife's death and nobody raises an eyebrow, but even a young widow's fate is sealed. There are of course laws to prevent dowry, wife abuse etc. Laws! My foot! This would go on and on."

In a way, Rajam was lucky that her in-laws insisted on her continuing her job as a teacher even after her marriage. It was hard work of course, right from 9 in the morning to evening 4'oclock. But it really gave her some footing, something to fall back upon when life played dirty tricks on her. Suddenly her mother's words were ringing in her ears. "Rajam, you should not touch a penny from your salary; that was meant for your marriage expenditure though it would only a drop-in the ocean."

The thought of her loving parents brought tears to her eyes. What hopes and aspirations they had, when they had agreed to pay an enormous amount of three lakhs as her dowry - a sum which they could ill-afford and would bring them literally to the street! Her father's Provident fund, the money her mother had earned from conducting music classes and saved with an iron will right from the time Rajam was born a quarter century ago plus her own earnings, had to be sunk for her marriage which lasted only a year but left her with painful and bitter memories for a life-time .

"What a disgrace! What an inhuman deal! Criminals, escaping scot-free. Who's there to question the wretched practice of dowry, the hurt and humiliation of a woman? What are these Sthree Seva Samajs, Mahila Raksha mandals and the other Women's' Organizations are doing in this country? They do hold Seminars and discussions on Dowry, Abuse of women etc. and a couple of big 'names' speak eloquently over delicious lunch and high teas and take processions always conscious of the flashing of TV cameras, while everyday thousands of dowry victims perish......" Rajam sighed deeply.
She realized that she could not escape from her haunting past, despite her sincere efforts.

Rajam remembered vividly the day when Sudarsan with his parents came for 'bride-viewing'. She was only too familiar with that scenario. The only room looked neat and tidy with the neighbor's four cane chairs occupying most of its space. The usual pyramid of mattresses, pillows and washed clothes on the corner had disappeared. Amma was in her old *'Kanchipuram '*sari with flowers around her hair while Appa was in his spotless white juba and dhoti, his fore-head shining with the traditional *'Iyengar'* mark. The aroma of the strong decoction coffee and the mouth-watering banana *bajjis* filled the air.

Rajam knew her role very well. She had to put on her pea-cock blue '*pattu*' sari; Amma would plait her hair and adorn it with jasmine flowers, all the time lamenting how thin and scanty her hair was. Rajam would not be allowed to use her glasses and she had to grope her way with coffee and snacks to the groom's party. Then she had to fall at the feet of the groom and his parents. Then, Appa would give a broad grin andnarrate enthusiastically Rajam's plus points to the groom's party, exactly like a salesman advertising his product.

"Rajam's an excellent cook, you see, she can prepare '*puliyodarai*' *extremely* well, that too very fast. Even my wife can't cook so deliciously. She's very intelligent too. Now, she's doing her B.Ed. by correspondence in Annamalai University.

Rajam sings very well, you must have heard of Trichy Parthasarathy Iyengar, the famous Carnatic musician, he was my father in law, my wife too sings, music's in their blood, you see?" Appa would continue after a pause, turning his grin to an artificial laughter, "Rajam, sing a song now?"

Then it was Rajam's turn to play the role of a meek and submissive daughter and sing to a disinterested audience.

After this 'bride-viewing", either they did not hear from the groom's party or a curt post-card letter would arrive expressing their 'inability to proceed' and wishing Rajam good luck.

Rajam was disgusted with her role-every time the same rejection, Amma's blaming it on Appa's looks and complexion she had inherited instead of her fair complexion and looks, Appa's meaningless consoling words about Rajam's good horoscope and the promise of a bright future. After every 'bride-seeing drama, Rajam felt extremely guilty for not only being born as a girl and a burden but also as a dark girl with no looks to her credit and not enough money to compensate her looks.

This had been happening at least thrice a month and Rajam had come to terms with the bride-viewing drama. She hardly looked up at the groom, the person with whom she had to share her life, for all of them were faceless, nameless men who did not matter to Rajam.........

So, when Amma said tenderly, "Come and have some hot coffee and get ready", instead of her usual harsh tone asking her to attend to the house-hold chores like 'Cut the vegetables' or sweep the floor", Rajam smiled. In fact she pitied her Amma's over anxiety to see her daughter married, the only goal for which she was born. "Amma, I'm tired, why can't you ask these people to come and 'inspect 'me' on..." before she could finish , Amma screamed, "How dare you?, today is an auspicious day-Friday. Moreover, you really think we can express our convenience, it's always theirs, the groom's party's convenience, go wash and come quickly wearing your *'pattu podavai'*, and I'll plait your hair; they'll be here by six.

Rajam obeyed her Amma's instructions and came back in her blue silk sari. Squatting in front of her Amma for plaiting her hair, Rajam thought, *'What an existence! Born to get married, that too after paying through nose to get a 'wife' status and go on with cooking, washing, bearing and rearing of children."*
"My God! You haven't removed your glasses yet. Remove it now, at once", Amma screamed.
"I've a head-ache. I'll remove my glasses as soon as I'm called for their 'appraisal', don't worry", said Rajam with unmistakable sarcasm.

Rajam acted her role in the bride-seeing drama, prostrated before the groom and his parents, served coffee and answered patiently all their queries regarding her age, job, pay etc.

Rajam had almost forgotten the episode, till much to her parents' delight, they got a letter from Varadachari, groom's father asking their convenience to discuss the details of the marriage.

The discussion followed and Rajam was shocked to hear that her father had agreed to pay Rs.4 lakhs in cash in addition to motor bike, refrigerator and a decent wedding and reception in the '*Kalyanamandapam* of their choice.

Wedding went off well and Rajam's father was spared the expenses of a music concert to entertain the guests as Rajam's auntie gave a music concert free.

Everybody praised Rajam's good fortune in getting an agreeable-looking, educated, impressive young man as her husband. Even Rajam could not help feeling a foolish thrill, when she had glimpses of her dhoti-clad husband in connection with the various elaborate rituals of the traditional Iyengar wedding.

Though Rajam was happy, she was quite apprehensive about the new life.
'Why did he agree to marry me, when he would've got a much better-looking girl? May be he was impressed by my song. Amma too was full of praise for my 'Kalyani' raagam that evening. Beauty is after all skin-deep. Thanks to Amma's training, I can cook well and am used to hard work. Further they seem to be a very broad-minded family as they want me to continue my job as a School-teacher."

Rajam cried uncontrollably, when she took leave from her parents. She was painfully aware of their sacrifices.

The price of her *managlasuthra* was their life-time savings. Mother had given Rajam even her pair of 'diamond' studs. When objected, Amma said, "You've no idea my child, diamond studs is a 'must' for an Iyengar bride. We can't afford to pay another lakh or more for this. This, I inherited from your *Paatti* and I can always wear white stone studs. Who bothers?"

Rajam suddenly felt very thirsty. She got up from her bed and switched on the light. Vanaja, her roommate was fast asleep. She envied her meaningful life as a lawyer helping out hundreds of 'victims' of marriage like her.

Vanaja often said, "You were a fool Rajam, An educated, thinking person like you, should not have given your consent for such a marriage. To imagine that your parents had to pay an enormous amount to buy a husband for their daughter and you had to suffer in silence for two long years..., you should have walked out on them, the moment they showed their true color....unbelievable!"

But, if she had to runway from her husband's house as Vanaja advised, she would have escaped from there after a week's stay.....

Lakshmi, Sudarsan's mother was absolutely devilish and ruled the house. Hardly a week after Rajam's arrival, she dismissed her part-time maid so that right from washing utensils to cooking became her responsibility. She had to get up very early to finish the house-hold chores before leaving for work.

On weekends Rajam had to grind rice and black gram daal in a grinding stone for the entire week, that too under the constant supervision and criticism of her mother-in-law. Once she suggested to her husband to get a grinder, he laughed villainously and said, "So, you think you need a grinder, no problem, ask your father to get you one, can't afford it right now,"

Another time, Rajam expressed her difficulty in finishing morning household chores before reaching the bus stop on time, pat came Sudarsan's reply, "As if you had many servants in your place, real Princess!"

In the beginning to keep herself from going insane, Rajam used to hum a tone while doing the monotonous, unpleasant household chores. Then, one day her mother-in-law reprimanded, "Enough of your songs, that's the only thing lacking. Your parents cheated us we didn't know that you're blind, yes, you can't see without glasses, better behave yourself."

Rajam had to hand over her entire pay to her mother in law and then had to depend on her even for her bus fare.

As far as Sudarsan was concerned Rajam was there to satisfy his lust. Sure, Sudarsan too, like Dr.Johnson believed that all women are the same in darkness. He married her, not because of her music as she had fancied. He knew, he did not have to take his wife around and his marriage in no way would affect his popularity among girl-students and female colleagues or his extra-curricular activities. She remembered bitterly how Sudarsan had once refused to bring her as his pillion rider on the bike he had bought from her Appa's money. When she requested him to pick her up after the School Anniversary, he laughed loudly and said, "You've hopes; you really think that I'll bring you in my motor-bike."

Sudarsan was highly irritable, short-tempered and even violent, at times.

Rajam was mortally afraid of her husband and mother-in law. Though her father-in-law was sympathetic, he never dared to protest against his wife's or son's cruel treatment towards a helpless girl.

Rajam felt miserable but could not confide in anyone her tales of woe. On a couple of occasions like Diwali or Pongal, Rajam's parents visited her, loaded with presents. But, she was not allowed to visit her home or contact them freely. Not that it would have made any difference. Once married, a woman belonged to her husband's home. She was brought up to believe in the sanctity of marriage and her duty to serve the 'lord and master' of her home. She was also conditioned to believe in sincere prayer. So, she prayed fervently to Lord Venkateswara, her family deity, for her husband's change of heart. But nothing happened.

In fact the situation became pathetic. Rajam lived in fear and could not sleep peacefully due to nightmares of her charred body. She often thought about the stories of 'bride-burning'.

"How do they do it? Do they really pour kerosene and set fire? This woman, this mother-in-law of mine is capable of doing that. She already starves me, if I fall sick and can't do all the donkey work or lose my job, she would really kill me. Further, if I die, they are the gainers. He can get married again and that means another couple of lakhs. Oh! My God! I'm frightened."

Then, that fateful day, the 24th of Feb, ironically her second wedding anniversary day, Rajam felt very feverish but did not dare to stay back and so went to her School. When she came back in the evening, she felt extremely dizzy and exhausted. Ignoring her mother-in-

law for the first time, she dragged herself to her bed room and lay there, her mind in a whirlpool.
Slowly, slowly, she closed her heavy eye-lids'.

"Ayyooo, don't kill me p-l-e-a-s-e, I don't want to die. Amma, don't look at me like that, I'm frightened, oh! You're going to pour kerosene, Ayyoo, I feel cold, very cold; stop it, s-t-o-p setting fire, and p-l-e-a-s-e… help, h-e-l-p-Ayyoo."

With great effort, Rajam opened her eyes and saw her mother in law pouring something on her body. A piercing scream escaped from her lips. Her head swimming with incoherent thoughts, she looked again and realized that her mother-in-law was pouring water on her to wake her up from her untimely sleep. But the damage was already done. Her delirious brain gave way and that resulted in voicing her worst fears.
That was the time her husband turned up. Rajam looked pleadingly at the man who tied the *mangalsuthra* and took seven steps around the sacred fire, exactly two years ago.

Sudarsan advanced towards her menacingly pushed her to the ground. Letting his mounting fury escape through filthy language, he started hitting her again andagain. Except for a neighbor's interference, Rajam would have been   beaten to death…….

Rajam looked at her watch and the time was well past midnight. Lost in thoughts, she had taken more than an hour to write a letter to her Appa. She hastily concluded her letter.

"Appa, don't worry about me anymore. My friend Vanaja is a Woman's rights lawyer and has already filed my 'Divorce petition', 'Divorce by mutual consent.' She also promised to get at least a part of the money you had spent on buying me a husband. Money would not be a problem for them as they could even get more dowry next time. Appa, our society is full of Sudarsans and Lakshmis. As long as there are parents like you and educated 'fools' like me, they would thrive.

I'm glad that I'm alive and what's more, sane in spite of my humiliating experiences. This's like a new lease of my life.

Tell Amma, I'm practicing my music every morning and even conduct music classes on weekends. My understanding Principal got me a substantial raise in pay with retrospective effect.

I'm sending you some money now. I'll come to spend my Diwali holidays with you both. Tell Amma I'm very happy in the company of sincere friends like Vanaja and well-wishers like my Principal, who actually restore my faith in humanity.

With lots of Love.
Yours
Rajam

SILVER WEDDING ANNIVERSARY

"Tomorrow I'm taking you all for dinner to Taj, be there by 8 and I'll join you, later I'm planning to go for a movie with my friends, okay?" said my son with a broad grin.

"We'll come, but I'll foot the bill, tomorrow is our silver wedding Anniversary, yes, twenty-fifth", declared my husband with a tinge of pride. I nodded in agreement.

"C'mon Appa, don't forget tomorrow is not only your wedding Anniversary but also my twenty-second birthday, so this time let me celebrate", insisted my son.

"What he says is true, for the past so many years, you've celebrated your wedding Anniversary and his birthday together. Now, give him a chance to celebrate both," my daughter interfered and the finality of her tone settled the matter.

The next evening I took special care to dress up, wore an ocean-blue *sambalpuri* sari, my husband's gift for the occasion and my husband looked years younger in his light brown *kurta pajama*. My daughter was at the wheel and my husband was next to her with his scrutinizing eyes on the heavy traffic. Seated at the back of the seat, my mind raced back to the 'Gandhi Jayanthi' day, second of October, 26 years ago, when I first met my husband under very strange circumstances.

At that time, I was a lecturer in Maharajah's College, actually converted from the palace of Maharajah of Vizianagaram inside a fort to a Women's College. As I was the warden of the Women's' Hostel inside the well-guarded fort, none could enter the premises without my permission. As second of October was a holiday, I was chatting with my friend, when I noticed the shocking sight of two young men parking their **Scooter inside and walking merrily inside the Hostel area.**

"Go away", I yelled at them presuming that they were students from the nearby Men's College. My words did not seem to bother them, instead of getting lost, one of them walked coolly towards me,
"Ma'am, I'm Lieutenant Krishnan and this's my friend Lt. Kumar." "This's a women's hostel", I told him.

"We didn't know that Ma'am", said Krishnan sounding as polite as I was rude. Our ships are nearby in Visakhapatnam and we were guided to this palace for sight–seeing; we are very, very sorry."

While I stared at him wondering if it was another tall story, Krishnan spoke again, "Ma'am forgive us our trespasses." I thought I saw a naughty twinkle in his eye.

His words made me smile; my anger suddenly gave way to admiration for the smart, gentlemanly officer. The next thing I did was to invite them to my quarters for tea. I even asked one of our attendants to take them around sight-seeing after tea.

Days later, I got a thank you note from Lieutenant Krishnan with an invitation to visit his ship with my friends.

The next Sunday we went on board INS Investigator, the first time I had been on a ship. And from then on it was a haze of letters that soon became phone calls, dates, stolen kisses, picnics on the beaches and of course our firm decision to get married....

But, I vividly remembered the tornado caused by our decision as we belonged to two different states and communities, I, a non-Brahmin from Kerala and he, a Brahmin from Tamil Nadu. Krishnan's family as well as mine swore that our marriage would not work.

We did not give in; we got married and proved them all wrong.

Twenty-five long years, crowded with so many unforgettable incidents, our simple marriage, brief honey moon, babies, frequent transfers, yes, the good and bad times of togetherness which seemed like events of yesterday, slipped by. Now, my angelic baby girl is a twenty-three old Doctor and my son, the priceless gift on my third wedding Anniversary, is flying to the US to do his Masters in Engineering. Time just flies, I heaved a deep sigh.

I deliberately brought back my mind to a few memorable wedding anniversaries.
We celebrated our first wedding Anniversary in Coonoor, but the 'flutter' inside me constantly reminded me that 'she 'would join us on our second Anniversary.

We 'three' had a grand celebration with brand new clothes for all of us and a grand dinner in Dehradun which of course had considerably upset our shoe-string budget, then.

We were in Cochin for our third and most memorable wedding anniversary. It was raining cats and dogs. When I developed labor pain at an unearthly hour, we went to the Naval Hospital. My husband waited outside with my one and a half year old, restless daughter. Within half an hour my' understanding' son arrived, reminding me of 'Olan's child-birth in 'Good Earth', yes, like that peasant woman I delivered my son with the help of a sleepy nurse.

Later so many of our wedding anniversaries passed by, sometimes we were together, some other times my husband away in his ship, But, we never forgot to celebrate the great day in whatever way we could.

I looked at my husband sitting in front seat, guiding my daughter in the traffic. His once thick mop of hair had thinned down considerably. He had put on weight. For that matter, I too had changed a lot. The slim, pretty girl in the NCC Uniform in our bed room was a complete stranger to me now. I did not know how my dream figure had transformed to enormous fat. My once flawless complexion was wrinkled now. Initially, when I noticed those laugh lines and when the loveliest of saris could not hide my fat, I was of course upset. But, slowly I came to terms with the inevitable onset of old age. But, despite all the havoc played by time, deep down we were the same. We loved each other more deeply than ever and longed for each other's company. Of course the old romance and excitement had given way to a more deep-rooted emotion. We felt the need for each other. A much stronger and more intimate emotion than love bound us together now. He had been the most caring, loving, husband, a perfect father to my children.

"Where're you, so lost in thought", C'mon get out of the car", my husband's voice brought me back to the present. Then, he gently led us to the reserved table inside the Hotel room. Soon, my son joined us.

All of us enjoyed the elaborate dinner with our favorite dishes followed by ice cream. An hour passed in a jiffy and then looking at his watch, my son got up and announced in a hurry, "Appa, I've to go with my friends for the movie, remember, I told you Suresh got tickets for all of us."

When my son was about to ride away in his motor bike, my husband got a brilliant idea. He had to raise his voice to make himself heard in the roaring noise of the bike.
"Why don't you take the car drop your sister in the Nursing Home for her night shift and pick up your friends for the movie? I'll take your mom for a Malayalam movie in your bike."
My son was only too happy to trade his bike for the car and happily our children drove off...

I was not at all puzzled by this last minute proposal of movie as I was so much used to my husband's on the spot decisions in the past.
But, my only concern about my husband's riding on my son's 'Yamaha'. Though my husband had a 'Bullet' about two decades ago, he must be quite out of touch. Still, I welcomed the idea as it was thrilling to go as his pillion rider after so many years, that too on our silver wedding anniversary.

"Don't you think I always get great ideas? It's fun to go like good old days on a bike and I know you love Malayalam movies. Let's go", my husband kicked the bike and it roared deafeningly. I carefully tucked my sari *palu* and sank into the seat. My husband managed to move through very unsteadily and we started our memorable trip to the theatre.

The theatre was only three kilometers from the Hotel and we had plenty of time. My husband went to the extreme left of the road and rode very, very slowly. I thought he was over-cautious as he was new to the bike. Suddenly, I noticed that he was holding the handles like a heavy weight champion lifting weight. He did not seem to change the gear or speed up. Soon, I saw buses, cycles and even pedestrians overtaking us. Embarrassed by the curious looks of the passersby, I asked, "What's happening? Can't you go faster? You don't seem to know how to ride this bike. Why did you ever think of such a silly idea?" I nearly screamed.

"Don't spoil my mood, you're quite heavy and I'll lose my balance. Isn't it nice to go slow? What's the big hurry; after all that 'Mammooty' film has been running here for the past two months and the theatre would be empty now. We've more than 40 minutes to reach the place which is hardly 3 kilometers from here."

I kept quiet for some time. Suddenly to my utter shock, I heard the screaming horn of the bike, which further attracted the attention of passersby. I could see them laughing at us. We must have been a perfect sight, my husband with his frying-pan like helmet and I with my sari tucked up so high to prevent from getting caught on the wheel, at snail's pace on a brand new, gleaming Yamaha.

"For Heaven's sake stop honking that damn horn, I yelled.

"Listen, I don't know how to switch on the indicator. Whenever I try to switch on the indicator, I happen to press the horn. It's all because of our son, he could've shown me. The moment I said "take the car", he drove off.

"Don't blame him for our pitiable condition. The moment you saw the motor bike you wanted to ride for re-living our past romance. I was a fool to let this happen. And I'm going to miss the beginning of that wonderful murder mystery. We might as well 'walk' on the bike home."

Irritated, my husband tried to look back and the bike wobbled I and I held him tightly.

"If you grumble like this, I'll get nervous and both of us will fall. I'm riding okay. I'm only being careful. After all, you can't expect me to ride like those days, we're getting old."

"You're not going to fool me by blaming it on old age. You simply don't know how to ride this bike. It's okay if I miss the first scene. I only hope that we would reach the theatre." I could not help laughing at his funny, awkward riding. I made a mental note of all his movements to relate to the children later.

After about half an hour, we reached the theatre. We certainly would have reached the theatre faster by walking.
Near the theatre- gate he asked me to get down as he could not maneuver   the bike inside among the row of neatly parked cars and bikes. He got down, took off his helmet and pushed clumsily the heavy bike, while I trotted along. Though miserable at being the laughing stock of everyone around, I was amused imagining the guffaw of children hearing our adventure.

After parking the bike, we got tickets and went inside the theatre. Once seated, my husband whispered triumphantly.

"See how I reached you on time; you haven't even missed advertisements."
I was too happy to dampen his enthusiasm by reminding him that we took more than half an hour to cover three kilometers.

We were so absorbed in the suspense movie that I almost forgot the ordeal of riding back home till the end.

Once the movie was over, my husband suggested that we would wait for all the vehicles to disappear before starting our journey back. We waited patiently till the last cycle left and rode back almost the same way as we rode to the theatre. The only difference was, this time I enjoyed every minute of the ride as the roads were practically empty and I was in no hurry. So, I clung to him as I used to, decades ago, when he cautiously rode through the ill-lit roads.

When we reached home, to our great shock, our son was pacing up and down the verandah. The moment he saw us, he came towards us running, "What happened, why are you so late? You gave me the fright, time is well past three and the movie must have been over a long time ago." A torrent of questions….
I could not help smiling at the reversal of roles. It was we in the past, waited anxiously outside, if our son did not turn up on time imagining all sorts of terrible things. Now, our son was grown up enough to be concerned about us.

My husband smiled charmingly and said, "Oh! You know we went to the beach and relaxed for some time. Since Sherry was away in her Nursing Home and you were with your friends, we thought of enjoying the cool, fresh sea breeze. After all, I'm a sailor and sea still is my first love. Sorry for making you anxious, son." He meaningfully winked at me...

I looked at my husband. Behind that thinning hair and slight paunch, I could see my husband of 25 years, the young man who had grown old with me who worked hard leaving behind his family to provide our children all possible comforts. All at once, I realized the cruel hands of time could only make physical changes but failed miserably to touch our beautiful, young spirit. I could still experience the thrill of our sitting together on the beach, twenty years ago, the excitement of my going as the pillion reader for the first time, the magic of the first stolen kiss, and million other details. Gratitude and affection filled my heart. I know each wedding anniversary brought new hope and new life. Each year-why, each dawn might bring a new struggle too - but as long as he is there I'm confident of coping with it.

DREAMS SHATTERED

Pushpa looked forward to Saturday evening. Saturdays filled her with expectations of her Amma going out, leaving her all by herself at night. Not that she was that lucky every Saturday; all depended on Sivamama coming with his cycle rickshaw to fetch Amma. Every day on Pushpa's way back home from the bungalow where she worked, she prayed in the Amman Kovil for Sivamama to come the next day. Of course, Saturdays meant additional work for Pushpa. But as long as Amma went out, she did not mind the trouble.

Pushpa had to help Amma for her elaborate head bath before going out; she had to collect water from the road-side hand-pump and then heat it. Heating water was always a time-consuming and tedious process. She had to arrange three huge bricks to make a stove, then collect dry twigs, coconut-shells, waste paper and blow on them with all her might to get the fire going to heat the water. When the water boiled, she had to pour in the right quantity of cold water to get the temperature just right; otherwise Amma would beat her up badly. She had to help her in bathing too which of course she enjoyed, as she could smell the soap she saw on TV in memsaab's bungalow. Her Amma had no sense of shame; she would stand in front of Pushpa with just a small loincloth around her waist, her firm breasts thrusting forward, her shapely thighs and arms exposed. Pushpa had to soap her body and apply shikakai to her lustrous black hair. Pushpa admired her Amma's hair and beauty. True, Amma was not fair-complexioned like her memsaab. She was dark, very dark, but she was slim and had very long hair. Her memsaab had very short, bobbed hair, like a boy. Though fair, she was fat, very fat, and moved clumsily. Pushpa admired her memsaab only when she drove her car. Sitting on the back seat, on their weekly drive to the market, Pushpa admired her memsaab's fair hands and fingers with their long, painted nails, turning the steering wheel this way and that way. But her Amma had slim, shapely hands with orange fingertips because she used mehndi so often.

If only her Amma could show her a little love and kindness! Memsaab was certainly kinder than her Amma. Though Pushpa had to work quite a lot in the bungalow, she was given food and for Diwali, a new blouse and *pavadai*. Memsaab even tipped her ten rupees whenever there were 'meetings' in her bungalow. True, on meeting days Pushpa had to do a lot of extra work, polishing the brass curios, taking trays laden with teacups and saucers and paper plates with snacks and sweets to the guests. The cook of the bungalow, who had passed his matriculation said, the meetings were very important and were meant to change the plight of women in society. He also said memsaab gave speeches and wrote in women's magazines about women's problems. Though Pushpa did not understand anything from the talk she happened to hear while serving tea, she knew it was all something great, as they always spoke in English, raising their squeaky voices.

Pushpa was really curious to know how these meetings changed the fate of women but she did not dare to ask the cook. If she annoyed the cook, he was powerful enough to deprive her of her usual quota of food. Between her memsaab and her Amma, Pushpa preferred memsaab. At least she did not beat her like her Amma did; she smiled at her after every meeting and said, "Thank you, Pushpa, here, take this money and go for a movie at your neighbor's house." Pushpa was lucky that those meetings in the bungalow generally coincided with her Amma's outings on Saturdays. Once she had helped Amma with her hot-water bath, Pushpa loved to watch her getting ready. After her bath, Amma would put talcum powder generously not only on her face but also on her armpits, stomach, in between her thighs and legs. She would put on her dark red blouse and yellow silk sari and stand before the oval-shaped mirror, adjusting her make-up; she would tie a red ribbon on her still-wet long hair, entwine a lot of jasmine blossoms around it, put a decorative sticker *bindi* on her forehead, pencil her arched eyebrows and apply *kajal* to her large, luminous eyes. She would even put on lipstick and then she would wait impatiently for the arrival of Sivamama and his cycle rickshaw. Finally, when Sivamama arrived, she would quickly remove the *managalsuthra* she wore on a yellow thread and would hide it in the old steel trunk. Pushpa always thought that Amma looked prettier without it because otherwise that dirty, thick, yellow thread on her neck hid her gold chain. Amma never forgot to give last-minute instructions to Pushpa.

"Pushpa, eat the rice and dry fish curry. Don't sleep off like a log. Get up early and collect water. Run to the pilot's flat and finish the work there before going to your bungalow. Take care not to annoy the pilot memsaab who's very finicky. If I hear any adverse report from her, I'll simply kill you, you know that, *Hah*?" Then she would add, "All because of that bastard, who left me and went off to Madurai," and she would go on and on till Sivamama screamed, "Enough of your instructions, come soon, Akka, we can't afford to make these rich people wait for us."

When Amma went, Pushpa heaved a sigh of relief and ran to her neighbor's house where, for two rupees, she could watch a Tamil movie on video. Pushpa did not know where Amma went or what she did. She was very happy that Amma would not return that night, so that she could watch the movie in peace. If Sivamama did not come on a Saturday, Pushpa would be the victim of Amma's wrath; she would beat her with whatever was available in the kitchen – broom, coconut-scraper, firewood. Once, she was beaten so badly that she could not even go to work for a couple of days. But she secretly enjoyed that time, because Amma had to do all the house work, right from collecting water from the pump to cooking rice gruel and dry fish at night. She was glad that she could at least then make her Amma realize the amount of work she had to do every day. Amma never lent her a helping hand. After finishing her part-time job in the Pilot's flat, she either indulged in gossip or ran to her neighbor's house to watch TV. Amma never took her for any of these sessions, was always cruel to her. She stopped her studies when she was barely six, took her along every day to the bungalow where she worked and trained her to do all her jobs. Though only thirteen, Pushpa was now an expert in the work. Her memsaab knew her worth; that was why she always made it a point to give her ten rupees after every meeting. Pushpa, of course, had to hide the money from Amma, or she would snatch it off from her.

Pushpa was inclined to believe the old woman in the next hut, who said that Amma was not her real mother. Whenever the old woman got a chance, she showed her toothless gums and said,
"Pushpa, that whore is not your mother; how can a mother be so cruel to her own child? She never gave birth to you, I'm sure of that. Next time you soap her dirty body, look for stretch marks on her tummy; there'll be nothing, I'm sure. No woman can have such a flat tummy and a figure like your Amma's after

delivery. I've been here for the past eleven years and I've never set eyes on her husband, your so-called father so far. God knows who tied that *thali* she wears*! Thoo, thoo!,"* she spat betel-stained, red-colored saliva. Pushpa guessed that was the truth. But she did not dare to ask Amma. Amma seemed to be always angry with her. However hard she tried to please her, Amma found fault with her, nearly starved her at night. She would say, "You eat the whole day in that bungalow. If you eat at night also, you won't work." If Amma went out, she could eat nicely, could be all by herself. She was not at all scared at night. She loved to keep awake, remembering the love scenes of Rajnikanth and Sridevi.

Pushpa liked Rajnikanth very much. She prayed in the *Amman Kovil* every day that she should get a husband like Rajnikanth. In one movie, Sridevi, the heroine, prayed all Fridays to the Goddess and the Goddess appeared before her and granted all her wishes. The Goddess looked more beautiful than the *Kovil Amman. Kovil Amman* was usually adorned with a *pavadai* of cheap, red cloth or with neem leaves. Pushpa did not like the jet- black idol. That *Amman* in the *Kovil* with her turmeric and vermilion resembled her Amma and the women in the neighboring huts. But, in the movie K.R. Vijaya was beautiful with her glittering jewelry and dark red zari sari. So, when Pushpa prayed she liked to recollect the Goddess' face in the movie. She prayed sincerely that her suffering should come to an end, she should get saris and jewelry like the Goddess and should get married to someone like Rajnikanth. She adored Rajnikanth, his hairstyle and his moustache and the way he talked, walked and danced around with Sridevi. Pushpa also wanted to live in a big bungalow, like the one in which she worked. She always admired the smooth, shining floors of the bungalow while swabbing them. Even the bathrooms looked very posh with showers and bathtubs.

She envied every woman who could wear silk saris, jewelry and live in posh bungalows, drive cars and order around servants. She knew that *Amman* was so powerful. Wouldn't she answer Pushpa's sincere prayers?

Then, one day the great event happened. That again was a Saturday. Pushpa felt very tired after her work in the bungalow. Since it was a 'meeting day' she had to polish the brass curios, change the cushion covers, vacuum the carpet, arrange the potted plants and wash innumerable cups and saucers. The cook had already warned her that the meeting was very important, that it would even be covered on TV. He said, memsaab and her friends were all protesting against the kidnapping and rape of a minor girl. Pushpa did not understand any of it; all she knew was that she had a lot of extra work. Moreover, the unusual excitement of the TV coverage had made her memsaab forget her usual tip of ten rupees. So Pushpa was slightly depressed. Added to that, she felt a sharp, shooting pain at the pit of her stomach. As soon as Pushpa reached her hut, she collected water, heated it and helped her Amma with bath and make up. Though she felt very uncomfortable she did not dare to express her uneasiness. Once Amma went away, she cried and cried, pressing her stomach with a pillow. Slowly she dozed off. When she got up a little later, she noticed blood stains on her white *pavadai*. Alarmed, she ran to the old woman next door and narrated the whole episode. Much to her annoyance, the old woman laughed and laughed opening her toothless mouth wider and wider. Pushpa had to shake the old woman, almost hurting her shoulders to stop her uncontrollable laughter. Then, in between laughter, the old woman nodded her head and said, "Good, good, *oh* ,that's it! I suspected it; even my ageing eyes could see the change in you. I was wondering why you're less ugly now-a-days, at times you even look pretty; your skeleton body is getting filled out fast, very good. So, my dear young girl's going to outsmart her Amma, her time has come, *ha ha.*" Then she added hastily, "Don't worry girl, you've become a big girl. All girls get blood like this once a month for about a week. Your good fortune has begun. Just you wait and see. From now on your Amma will give you all the love, affection and care in the world. This old woman doesn't lie."

Pushpa did not believe the old woman, then. But it was true. In the morning, when Amma came, she made all the fuss in the world about Pushpa's illness. Pushpa was given raw egg in milk, jaggery and bananas. She was even asked to rest. In a voice filled with affection, love and care, her Amma said, "You don't go to work for three days, we've to celebrate your becoming a big girl. I must ask at least two month's advance from your memsaab, I'll buy you a new *pavadai, davani* set."

Pushpa had a wonderful time. For three long days she was treated like a queen. Amma too took leave for a couple of days to attend to her. She was given rice, fresh fish curry and sweets. Amma invited a few of her friends including the old woman for lunch. That Saturday, when Sivamama came to pick Amma up she said something in hushed tones to him and they both guffawed. Mama then pinched Pushpa's cheek and said, "Hey Pushpa, big girl, I'll get you a present next time when I visit you." Everything was like a dream. True to her word, Amma bought her a red blouse, a long red skirt with white polka dots on it and a red silk half-sari. Pushpa was excited beyond words; this was the first time she'd ever got a brand new dress. All these years, she had worn the discarded dresses from the pilot's daughter, who was tall and rather on the fat side. Naturally, Pushpa in her ill-fitting clothes was a source of constant amusement to all. Dressed up in her new dress, her hair oiled, plaited and decorated with jasmine buds, she even watched a Rajnikanth-Sridevi movie. In the merry-making, Pushpa forgot all her discomfort, the nasty trickling of blood and the severe cramps in her stomach. In fact ,she enjoyed her new status and the attention she got from every one. Amma told her she should not pray or stand near the *Kovil* when she got the same trouble next month as it would lead to Amman's wrath. Pushpa could not understand why Amman should get angry with her, if she went to the *Kovil* on those days but she decided to obey the command of her infallible Amma.

A couple of months passed and one fine day, Pushpa's prayers were answered. A young man who looked just like Rajnikanth came to her hut. Sivamama brought him along with him. When that man looked her up and down with his piercing eyes, Pushpa blushed. He looked every inch a hero, just like Rajnikanth, the same hairstyle, the same mannerisms. Pushpa was thrilled by the hero's presence in her humble hut. When, Amma and Sivamama left for some shopping, leaving Pushpa alone with the hero, she was ecstatic. Slowly, just like in his film, Rajnikanth approached her and held her close to him. She was so scared that he could hear the loud pounding of her heart. She looked down, half-closed her eyes. She was afraid to look up and break the spell. He slowly put his hand under her chin and raised her face, pleading with her to open her beautiful eyes and look at him. She opened her eyes and their eyes met. He pulled her closer to him and kissed her on her lips. She felt his exploring fingers all over her body. She heard him saying over and over again, "You're beautiful, don't feel shy, look up, look at me, don't you like me?"

"Of course I like you, I love you, I adore you, you are the man of my dreams, my prince, my lord, my Rajnikanth, and I'm your slave. Amman has answered my prayers at last", she wanted to say, but the words stuck to her lips. It was sheer ecstasy.

It was incredible, how much and how quickly Pushpa changed after that night. She was in a world of her own, a world in which no one existed except she and Rajnikanth. Holding the small mirror in her hand, she examined each part of her body which she had surrendered so totally to her lord. She realized for the first time that she exuded an unusual charm. She had a shining, flawless complexion. Her eyes sparkled with kajal, and the white stones clustered like a shining bee on her right nostril, gave a special charm to her straight nose. She also noticed a sexy cleft dividing her chin. She wore a new string of pearls, a pair of pearl earrings and lots of glass bangles which Rajnikanth himself brought for her. She was the happiest girl on earth now, none could mar her happiness. Next weekend, her prince said he would take her to Bombay, his work place and leave her for a while with his aunt. Pushpa wanted to discuss the details of their marriage but was too shy to ask. Further, she did not want to break the short magic spell provided by Amma's absence.

Pushpa's Amma too changed a lot. She not only did not beat her, but also was very kind. Amma's old trunk was polished and neatly packed with red, blue, green and yellow synthetic saris with matching blouses and petticoats, padded brassieres, powder, new slippers and lots of fake jewelry. Pushpa knew that it was not Amma's money that was spent so lavishly on her; Amma was generous with Rajnikanth's money, probably given with special instructions to equip his bride-to-be. Pushpa saw with her own eyes, Rajnikanth handing over bundles of currency, she had no idea how much. Neither did she care to find out. She was in a dream world where nothing mattered. At last *Amman* had answered all her prayers and she was going to get a rich, loving, caring, fashionably dressed husband.

When Pushpa took her leave from the old woman, she shook her head and said, "I wish you could stay back child, but you can't. This old woman's eyes can't see clearly anymore but I guess you're charming and young and, after all, Mother Nature is very generous to every woman at your age. As they say, even a donkey will be beautiful at sixteen. But, pretty looks and an illiterate orphan girl is no good combination, my child." Pushpa did not bother to listen much to the old woman's gibberish. As Amma correctly said, she certainly was a jealous old hag.

In the train, Rajnikanth and Pushpa sat in separate compartments. As instructed by her lord, she did not talk to anyone on the long journey; neither did she miss anyone at home. She was in fact very happy to leave behind the wretched hut, the starvation, Amma's beatings and the drudgery in the bungalow. Though Amma had changed in the past two months, Pushpa simply could not rely on that change which could very well be a temporary one. Actually, she considered herself very lucky to have come away that too with a man she adored.

In the hotel room in Bombay, Pushpa was very happy. She surveyed the small, cozy bedroom with its twin beds, soft mattresses, and attached bathroom with bathtub and shower. Extremely pleased with her dream room, she removed her clothes in a jiffy and ran to the bathroom for a nice shower. She loved the feeling of hot water trickling down from the shower over her tired body, making her fresh and energetic. She reminisced about her pleasant experiences after Rajnikanth came into her life and felt that all her dreams had come true.

She could not help humming a tune from a popular Tamil movie, *"chinna chinna asai'*....

When she heard Rajnikanth's footsteps, she hastily draped a towel around herself and ran to the adjoining bedroom, water dripping from her body everywhere. Then, quite unexpectedly, Pushpa saw through the corner of her eye, Rajnikanth pulling out a bottle of liquor from a brown packet. Sitting on the edge of the bed, he almost ordered Pushpa to fetch a glass from the table. When she hesitated, he said in his gruff voice, "Haven't you seen in the movies, your hero Rajnikanth drinking, *eh*? The only difference is, I don't dance around the tree chasing you and the music is from the TV, my sweet heart?" And he laughed loudly. …

After a few drinks, Rajnikanth pulled Pushpa to the bed and made love to her, until all the accumulated lust was drained out of his system. She wondered what happened, why he was in such a hurry to have sex, without a word of affection or endearment. He did not comment on her beautiful figure or say a word about their impending marriage. All he said after love-making, in a matter-of-fact tone, was, "Be a good girl and behave yourself in my aunt's place, there will be more girls like you. They talk mostly Hindi, never mind, my aunt knows a bit of Tamil. I'll visit you every now and then; after all I have successfully initiated you into the dream world, dear – really a unique honor, my sweetheart". He laughed louder and louder. After a while, a bewildered Pushpa could hear his snoring.

Pushpa lay awake for a long time beside Rajnikanth. Her head throbbed and her body ached. Slowly, slowly she closed her eyes. She saw a handsome, smiling, singing Rajnikanth whirling her off her feet, kissing her all over, his hands exploring the perfect curves of her body. She writhed with pleasure. But suddenly her

Rajnikanth became a hairy man, double his original size, smelling of alcohol, suffocating her and trying to murder her in his embrace. She tried in vain to free herself. She prayed to *Amman,* the black idol in the *Kovil,* to help her, but the idol's face changed into K.R.Vijaya's smiling beatifically, just like in the movies. "Is this really happening to me? Is this a fact or fantasy, a dream or reality?" Pushpa tried hard to remember, but her confused brain refused to give any clue, though the reality was snoring blissfully beside her.

THE KEY TO THE GATES OF HEAVEN

Savy's frenzied fingers moved on and on while her mind raced back to her past, dredging out memories she deliberately wanted to forget. But she marveled at her capacity to unravel the mystery covering a span of twenty long years without any emotion, as though it was all happening to someone else. Perhaps, she developed this strange immunity due to her survival instinct; otherwise how could she bare her soul to a stranger on the other side of the globe? *Stranger*? Huh! How could she ever consider her daughter, her own flesh and blood, her 'Kutty Malu', a stranger? Was it easy to sever the magic bond of mother-daughter relationship like the umbilical cord?

Savy remembered, her life was nothing but a string of seemingly unimportant events, an unbroken chain of strange coincidences, otherwise how could she account for her latest chance encounter with Mayura, an intern in New York's Lennox Hill Hospital, that too, in a small veterinary clinic in the suburbs of Chennai? And how could Mayura find the uncanny resemblance between the stranger Sabithri Banerji, sitting next to her and her close friend in New York, Malavika Menon?

Savy, deliberately brought her mind back to the inauguration of the Arts Club of Maharajah's College, Ernakulam a quarter century ago. Clad in an off white sari with zari border, her ankle length hair in a tight pony tail, Savy enthralled the audience with a semi-classical, Malayalam song. Later, when she received the Trophy from the Governor, she could almost feel the admiring eyes of the young, smart, Lieutenant, the

ADC to the Governor. Ignoring the loud drum beats in her heart, she walked away as if it was a pleasant dream......

Soon the dream turned into a nightmare for Savy when everyone started noticing Menon's motor bike hovering around the Women's College area, daily. She dreaded a scandal connecting her with an attention-getter, rich guy, which would sure break her poor, widowed mother Meenakshyamma's heart. She knew only too well that the miserable life of her mother revolved around her daughter's settling down with a suitable, loving husband, after her graduation.

One evening, with that middle- class- morality-induced courage, Savy confronted Menon.
"What do you take me for? Why are you following me, please stop this practice right now and at once, clear, c-l-e-a-r? "
The closeness of the most attractive, innocent face with a pair of hauntingly beautiful, luminous eyes flashing fire, unnerved Menon for a second. But recovering from the initial shock, Menon smiled, then broke into a shoulder-shaking laughter giving the impression that his shoulders were laughing. Savy could not help noticing his fine set of teeth and the curves around his lips, transforming his cherubic face with slightly receding hair instantly to an innocent school boy's ,while caught for punishment. Her anger suddenly gave way to admiration for the polite, smart, gentlemanly Officer.

"Kutty, you would agree with me that this College Campus is not an ideal place for confrontation', said Menon, sounding as polite as she was rude, "C'mon, hop in, let's go to the 'India Coffee house'. Sure, I need a strong cup of coffee to defend myself." Menon laughed again. Looking back, Savy did not know how and why she had agreed to go with him, that too as his pillion rider.........

Over a cup of coffee, Menon expressed his honest intention of marrying her with surprising eloquence for his usual, quiet, man-of-few words image. "Kutty, you stole my heart the moment you came to the stage, a month ago? I never felt this, *uh*, this, this..." Menon searched for the right word, and added, "This feeling for any other girl in my life. I love you, want to share the rest of my life with you. If you just say you like me, you don't mind marrying me, that's enough for now. If you agree, we can get married in a couple of months, before I go to Bombay on transfer."

Amidst the unforgettable three weeks' of hurried phone calls , a couple of visits to Savy's house to convince Meenakshyamma and of course the tsunami of opposition from the matriarch of a wealthy illustrious family, Menon's mother and her powerful bureaucrat brother, Menon married Savy in a simple ceremony in Guruvayur temple. .....

Though tears did not sting her eyes, Savy felt a heavy lump in her throat -- the memories of forgotten years ...her loving husband and his endless efforts to transform her to a sophisticated, incredibly charming Naval wife, the object of every one's admiration, their happy married life..

Savy remembered, how the news of Malavika's birth, had brought Menon's mother to Bombay and how she had adored her angelic granddaughter. Though she could not completely forgive Savy for snatching away her only son, '*my Babu*' ,as she had referred to Menon, she made every effort to be civil to her daughter- in - law during her frequent visits to Bombay, just to be with her adorable granddaughter.

For Savy's Amma, Mala was pure bliss, *'So, you're, 'Mala' for your Achan, Achamma, Kuttymalu for your Amma and for me, Kannamma; you know, 'kannu' means 'Eyes' in Malayalam and you've inherited your Amma's beautiful, sparkling eyes. Would you object to my calling you Kannamma when you grow up and become 'Little Miss India'?"* Meenakshyamma cooed, while bathing the baby.

But, alas, it was not to be, Meenakshyamma passed away peacefully in her sleep, when Kutty Malu was barely eight months..........

'Amma was lucky to escape this world right on time, before witnessing her daughter falling into this inescapable hell'. ....

Sighing deeply, Savy remembered that it was on Kutty Malu's third birthday, she first set eyes on the very young, debonair Lt. Banerji. Though Menon, the commanding Officer of INS Shanthi', mentioned the new addition to his ship, a very young and smart Lt. Banerji, Savy never expected him to be so handsome and boyish-looking.

As though justifying his looks, Lt. Banerji spent all his time with the birthday girl Mala and her young friends, taking pictures, conducting games, singing etc. Finally, 'uncle Banerji' entertained the exhausted kids by bringing alive the 'jungle world', with his superb mimicking of cawing cows, clucking hens, cooing parrots, mewing cats and barking dogs.

Both Menon and Savy were extremely grateful to the 'young hero 'of the evening. A generally reserved Menon, who gave the false impression of being unapproachable, could not help praising Amit Banerji for not only entertaining the kids but also taking full control of some of the older children especially the known bully, nine-year old Vikram, their neighbor's son.

Promising an adamant, unwilling Mala that he would come next weekend, Banerji was about to leave, when Menon suggested, 'Savy, why can't Amit have dinner with us?" then turning to Amit, he added, 'Amit, I'm a strict vegetarian unlike my wife and daughter, who can't eat a single morsel without fish, so, Savy always has some fish in the fridge, right Savy?'

Concealing her annoyance at this unexpected invitation, Savy quickly added, 'I was about to ask Lt. Banerji to come for lunch on Sunday. Never mind, you're most welcome now too, if you don't mind I've fish curry made in typical Kerala style, I can fry some marinated king fish too, so, join us' , said Savy walking towards the kitchen....."

Banerji enjoyed the viciously red, hot, fish curry and rice and praised Savy to the skies.
"Mrs. Menon's a great cook but since you're a pure vegetarian, there must've been some other way to your heart, not cooking, right Sir?"

"Oh, ours is not exactly a very romantic story, it's love at first sight, for me", stressing the word 'ME', he continued, 'I happened to hear Savy singing in their Arts Club inauguration, while I was also on the stage as the ADC to the Governor of Kerala. Within a month we got married in Guruvayur, that's all, not very romantic eh?" Menon laughed, shaking his shoulders.

"*Huh!* So, it's Mrs. Menon's music, that's very romantic, Sir, as the Bard says 'if music is the food of life, play on". Today Mrs. Menon is tired and I've to wait till Sunday lunch, to hear Mrs. Menon singing, how sad!" Everyone laughed, including little Mala.

Enjoying Sunday lunch and the special dish *'fish molie',* Banerji said, "Why don't you call me Amit, like Sir, that's more like home, actually I'm at home here except for that 'Banerji' bit?"

Savy promptly replied, 'Okay, then call me *'Didi'*, Amit'.

Amit looked up and for a split second, his eyes met Savy's and Amit said, "I can't call you *Didi*, you must be younger, so I'll call you 'Sabi', we, Bengalis say 'b' instead of 'v" okay?'

"*Oh!* You made my day, thanks Amit", Savy broke into peals of laughter, sending electric waves through Amit's spine.

From then on every Saturday loaded with gifts for little Mala, Amit accompanied the Menons to the Gymkhana club. While a grateful Menon enjoyed his *'Tombola'* with a couple of scotches uninterrupted, Savy enjoyed the handsome, young man's unconcealed admiration for her and affection for Mala.

Soon, Sunday lunch at Menon's place was followed by Savy's songs and Amit's watching English films with Savy, when Menon napped with a tired Mala………..

In less than a month, Menon's dream came true with his selection for submarine training in Russia. But the initial enthusiasm was considerably dampened due to his mother's refusal to come and stay in Bombay, that too, with the lame excuse of her *Ayurvedic* treatment in Kerala.

But convinced thoroughly by Amit's repeated reassurance that it was his duty to look after Menon's family as his own elder brother's, Menon bid a tearful farewell to Mala, Savy and Amit.

As promised to Menon, Amit started visiting Savy and Mala daily and either stayed back for Savy's delicious non-vegetarian dinner or took them out to posh restaurants.

Savy, no doubt, was changing though unwilling to accept that even to herself - a sort of Narcissistic, frequenting beauty parlor, always wearing transparent georgette saris which accentuated her curves, dieting , exercising etc. Her efforts of course were amply rewarded as she could feel the admiring glances of Amit followed by a shower of compliments, invariably resulting in her violent heart beats.

Then one fateful Sunday night while watching "Roman Holiday', Amit said, "You know Sabi, you look very much like 'Audrey Hepburn', he paused, moving closer to Savy and gently running his fingers through her lustrous hair, continued, his voice dropping to a whisper, 'except for your ankle-length hair. If you chop off your hair and wear jeans and shirts, you can be mistaken for 'Audrey Hepburn'. C'mon, Look at me Sabi, I mean it".

Savy did not move away, instead, she rested her head on Amit's shoulders, inhaling his faint, masculine perfume, listening to her own loud heart beats for a moment. Next moment, she was in his arms, her slender arms enveloping him, responding to his mouth, lips and tongue. Moaning with pleasure, she guided his feverish fingers to explore every part of her body. She did not say anything but language was superfluous, she let him know that she never experienced this ecstasy; their bodies dancing to a rhythm dictated by Anatomy, they lay in the sofa, her fair skin against his wheatish skin, her soft rose petal body against his hard body, her firm full breasts against his broad, hairy chest......

That Sunday's ecstatic experience was just the beginning of a never-ending whirl wind of romance of several months. But both Savy and Amit had no regrets; in fact they were happy to recognize the truth----- their fatal attraction was hopelessly linked up with libidinal drive. In that moment of recognition, their past, present and future faded away.

A thousand tongues wagged about Savy's sudden, almost unrecognizable metamorphosis from a respectable Naval Officer's wife, to a bob haired, glamorous, seductress, reveling in Amit's attention. Savy ignored the gossip, she was in a different world where nothing else mattered, except Amit's love and none else existed, except Amit......

But Menon's brief letter dropped the first bombshell -- his mother's arrival the following weekend with the intention of staying with Menon for the rest of her life.

Crying inconsolably, Savy told Amit her only option, 'suicide'. She just could not face Menon's mother and dread her visit as much as Menon's.

Wiping Savy's tears, Amit kissed her gently, laid her down whispering, "How could you think of suicide? I love you Sabi, you just relax, let me fix a drink", he walked towards the fridge. Later, after a couple of drinks and a hurried lovemaking, Amit left.

That night, tossing and turning in his bed, Amit cursed himself for his indiscretion, his dangerous liaison with a Senior Officer's wife. Unrepentant, he hated Savy's seducing him every possible way, *"After all I'm a man, and she purposely led me to this hell. I didn't rape her, she wanted this badly, expected it right from day one. Now, threatening with suicide, huh! Already my Senior Officers look at me with contempt, talk to me in threatening tone, what did her idiotic husband think of me, a gay, when he forced me to visit his house every day?"*

But deep inside, Amit was scared stiff of Savy's suicide threat which reminded him of an alcoholic Senior Officer's wife's suicide by setting herself ablaze ,in Cochin. Ignoring his wife's usual suicide-threat that Officer went to the Naval Mess and by the time he returned, she was succumbed to burns. *"These bold Malayalee bitches"*, Amit muttered aloud, clenching his teeth.

Next morning greeted Amit with the nerve-shattering news, his transfer order to Andaman Islands - a discreet punishment – transfer for tarnishing the image of the Indian Navy!

That was the time, Amit planned carefully every move to save his life and career, by eloping with Savy. As planned, Savy packed up her suitcase with jewelry and cash (*'to meet the initial expenses darling',* Amit said,) left her KuttyMalu with Menon's cousin, who was supposed to pick up her mother-in-law from the station.

Torn by the magnitude of her guilt, Savy cried inconsolably. Controlling his urge to strangle the weeping temptresses, Amit muttered some consoling words, patting Savy's back indifferently.

Looking back, Savy realized that the crack in the idyll of their relationship appeared on the very first night of their life together.

Days and months crawled by witnessing the transition of the charming, bubbly Mrs. Savithry Menon to a very quiet, much older–looking, pitiable Mrs. Sabithry Banerji, a mute witness to her handsome, young husband's making advances to attractive girls. Turning into a monstrous, suspicious bully, Amit, that 'model of geniality' did not spare Savy from questioning her relationship even with the domestics labeling her as a 'Nymphomaniac'.

Once in a big party hosted by the Captain of a Merchant ship, Amit, in his drunken stupor kissed his dancing partner, a pretty air-hostess, passionately on her lips in front of a jeering crowd.

Later, when Savy protested, Amit came towards her maniacally. With clenching teeth he thundered, "Shut up, don't provoke me to hit you, just one hit, you, sickly woman, would die and I'll be in jail. How dare you accuse me after ruining my life and my career? Your ex-husband Menon is now a hero with a great job in Naval attaché, enjoying his life like a blooming bachelor, while I'm accused as a wife-snatcher, breaking the sacred tradition of the Indian Navy, all because you seduced me to satisfy your accumulated lust. You can get out and mind you, I'm not going to buy your suicide-threat anymore. Go ahead, commit suicide, this 'hurt-wife' role doesn't suit you, darling!", expressing his uncontrollable fury through his flaring up nostrils, and curling upper lip, Amit said with unmistakable sarcasm.

After such fierce fights and most cruel accusations, Amit would apologize and promise not to repeat the brutal treatment. But, soon Savy realized that these promises were a routine affair, a means of gaining access to her body. Savy would not deny him the access, her only means to communicate to her husband, but could not respond to the ugly, unclean act of love-making with a man who hated her.

So, on one side lay a bad marriage, some semblance of security and an acceptance by society. On the other side lay the strange, alien and hostile world with a frighteningly oppressive, male-oriented society, especially for a woman who had been not only just a house wife for several years, but also the worst transgressor breaking the 'love-laws' of the society, who should love whom, how and how much……..

Letting out a deep sigh, Savy surveyed the spectacular display of wealth around - the spacious living room with leather-upholstered sofas, Kashmiri carpet, display cabinet with Swarovski crystal curios, a splendid chandelier and on one end of the living room, the wide, winding staircase with a polished banister and red-carpeted steps and on the other end, a bar with granite counter and an ornate glass cabinet in the rear, displaying choicest drinks - how Amit's life had changed dramatically, almost from rags to riches when his notoriously corrupt, womanizer, 'Uncle Biswas', Biswas Banerji, became the Union Defense minister!

In the blink of an eye, Biswas Banerji got his nephew out of the Indian Navy, made him his trusted Lieutenant to manage his flourishing Business Empire. The ruthless, power-crazy politician wanted exactly someone like Amit Banerji, unscrupulous, brainy and impressive 'smiling villain', to look after his shady Business interests when he was busy 'serving the people of India'. No wonder, the honorable Defense minister rewarded his nephew with a huge bungalow, fancy cars, spacious Office with a bevy of beauties at his beck and call, frequent trips abroad etc.

Savy slowly withdrew into a world of her own, with her beloved, understanding companion, 'Diana', a brown Doberman bitch. And the strangest of all coincidences in Savy's life, that fatal, chance encounter with Mayura, her KuttyMalu's friend, happened in the Pet Clinic, where Diana was taken for Vaccination...

The musical chiming of the multi-colored Swarovski-crystal clock brought Savy back to the present reality. She realized, she took three hours to cover a span of twenty long years of her life, *'only twenty years, seems an eternity'*. But, she was happy that she could write 'her story so far' without any emotion, except that chocking sensation, the thickening of that lump in her throat.

Looking at the long letter to be posted to Dr. Menon of Lenox Hill Hospital in New York, Savy, for the first time, stopped to think of her intention, the purpose of sharing the story of her life with a stranger.

'Stranger', *your own daughter, your own darling KuttyMalu a stranger?'*, an inner voice reprimanded *'So, you claim to be the mother of Dr. Menon? Impossible, her beautiful mom 'Savithry kutty' died in a car accident years ago while Commander Menon escaped, unhurt. A grief-stricken Menon remained a widower for the sake of his daughter and Malavika's Achamma, her Dad's mom, brought her up ,with much more love and affection than her own mom would have done . A picture perfect family,"* according to Mayura....

Sighing deeply, Savy shredded the long letter into hundreds of tiny bits and staggered towards her bed room with a dizzy feeling. Lying on her soft bed, Savy closed her tired eyes and clutched her throat to prevent the massive lump from spreading down.

"Wages of sin is death''; Savy could hear distinctly the loud voice of the Pentecost Preacher from her Maharajah's College junction. Frightened, she listened breathlessly......

Savithrykutty, open your eyes, your beautiful eyes, just like your daughter Kannamma's eyes and mine. Believe me, believe your own Amma, that Preacher is wrong. 'Moley', 'Wages of sin is not death; it is living, living in this hell like you're doing now. Death is beautiful, the golden panacea for your haunting memories. Yes, death is the key to Heaven, enough of this life, come, 'Moley', come, I've been waiting for a very long time to hold you, hug you and kiss you. Savithrykutty, open your eyes and look at me, your Amma."

Savy opened her eyes and clearly saw her Amma, white sari-clad Meenakshyamma, her wet, curly hair falling over her cheeks, fore-head adorned with a small line of sandal paste from the temple, standing with outstretched hands, in front of her. Savy could inhale the fragrance of fresh 'thulsi' leaves, sandal paste and camphor.
"Amma, I'm coming, I'm coming" Savy muttered aloud.......

I WANT TO BE LIKE 'KUTTAPPAN'

Abhay was enjoying his early dinner, cheese-filled pizza, carefully holding the edges of it and chewing noiselessly, with his mouth tightly closed. He usually had his dinner at well past eight, but that night was different, his parents wanted him to go to bed at eight so that, he could get up early next morning and get ready for his Telecast.

"You should finish your milk too after pizza and sleep off early, darling." An over-smiling Neethu reminded her son. "You know this telecast is not like the previous ones, it's very, very important. The whole country is going to watch this", she gently shook the back of Abhay's head and continued, "To get into the Guinness Book of world record is not an ordinary thing my son, you are the first five year old boy, to get this rare honour. Your Dad and I are so proud of you, sweetie pie" Neethu cooed in a voice filled with extra affection and love, nudging her husband.

Dr. Menon, seated next to her but busy going through his paper to be presented at the Cardiology conference in New York, took the hint, forced a smile and said in an unusually kind and persuasive tone .
"Yes, Abhay, we're so proud of you, Finish your food and go to bed early, okay, you're going to get a lot of surprise gifts from America, when we both come back"; then looking at Neethu, Menon added, "What a pity, we won't be here to see the telecast! We can of course watch it later, but we're going to miss the reactions of everyone, by the time we come back every one would forget Abhay's telecast. Ah, that reminds me, ask

Malini to pack up Abhay's clothes, favourite cartoons, toys, books etc. for two weeks"

"I'm worried about his Piano practice for the Annual Recital and Karate classes , luckily the missing school lessons were already taught in advance by his tuition teacher, that's the advantage of getting his Class teacher for tuition too , though she charges exorbitant fee for coming over here," sighing deeply, Neethu added, 'I'm also concerned about his stay with your parents in that God-forsaken place and his playing merry hell with that Kuttappan all the time , wish your mom had exercised some control over these low class people! She treats that boy like her own grandson, remember, how he used to be in your parent's place watching TV on all weekends, disgusting", she curled her lips contemptuously.

"Come on Neethu, my mother misses Abhay, she's very much attached to him, so she finds some pleasure in the company of that boy, what's his name," knitting his bushy eyebrows, pretending to remember the name, but actually gaining time to hide his annoyance at Neethu's comments, Menon continued, "oh yah, Kuttappan', what's more, Abhay would be happy to watch the telecast with my parents and Kuttappan there"

Suddenly Abhay jumped and threw his hands ceiling-wards and screamed with his mouthful of pizza, "*Yeeahaaaaaaha,* I'll be in Ammomma's place when you both go to New York, great fun!!!"

Both, Dr. Vijay Menon, a renowned Cardiologist in Chennai and his pretty Gynecologist wife Dr. Neethu Menon, were momentarily stunned by Abhay's sudden, unexpected and unconcealed enthusiasm and joy at his spending time in a remote place in Kerala, with Menon's parents. Recovering fast from the initial shock, Neethu was the first one to react, 'Behave yourself Abhay, how many times have I told you not to talk with your mouthful? Wipe that cheese off your cheeks with the serviette and *ssssit ddddown* and *eeeat* your pizza. Oh yeah, great fun to be with that urchin Kuttappan, no school, no piano, no karate, no tuition, twenty-four hours playing wild in the hot sun, no sense of propriety for our little celebrity'.

Abhay sat down quickly and with his head bent low, mumbled 'sorry, mom' and started nibbling at his pizza.

Menon's heart went out for his son, 'Abhay, the five year old child prodigy', as newspapers called him, who won several accolades for his amazing special talent to recite two tragedies of Shakespeare, Hamlet and Othello, in perfect BBC accent with proper expressions and voice modulations before packed audiences right from the time he completed his fourth birth day. Menon knew only too well, that it was Neethu who had discovered the unique talent of their son, nurtured and developed it to this level. Why Abhay's, even for his own success, Neethu the only child of a fabulously wealthy parents, was instrumental. As she often reminded him, except for her father's immense wealth, political influence and high connections, he would have been just another Cardiologist in Chennai. Menon was painfully aware of this fact and never tried to prevent an over-ambitious Neethu from what she wanted to do. He was of course proud of his son, who was dressed up, talked and behaved like a 'mini adult', but always wondered whether Abhay was actually enjoying his celebrity status. Wasn't he missing out on his carefree, innocent childhood? Whenever Menon voiced his doubts, Neethu silenced him by saying that, he would never, ever understand the present, highly competitive world, where rare achievement alone was the magic mantra for instant fame and success.

"You don't understand, Vijay, the present trend, you must be thankful that I'm here to promote Abhay's exceptional skill. What if I had not chanced upon his great ability to memorize, when I had taken him for those drama rehearsals? Then he was just two and seven months old and I still remember, how indifferent you were, when I appointed Miss. Mitchell to teach him English poetry and Shakespeare at that tender age. Now see the results. I don't deny that later you too took interest in Abhay's stage performances and tutored him for interviews, press meets etc, but that's all later, very much L.A.T.E.R. Don't forget, it's I, who discovered his talent initially. Abhay has my genes, you yourself admit that, I too had, why, still have a photographic memory; but my parents were only interested in seeing me with white coat and stethoscope and so pushed me towards that. Well, I'm glad that Abhay could achieve what I could not and I can at least bask in his glory'.

Menon knew from experience that, agreeing with Neethu was the only way he could stop her from the long monologue of comparison of his village background with that of her sophisticated upbringing in metropolitan cities.

Menon had to agree that, it was Neethu's discovery of Abhay's extraordinary memory power three years ago during his acting in an English Drama, had culminated in his rare and great achievement today. Abhay had been selected by a famous theatre group to act in their play, after interviewing many boys of two to three age group in reputed play Schools. The drama was centered around the legal battle of a very wealthy divorced couple about the custody of their two and a half year old son. During a fortnight's rehearsals to which Neethu had taken Abhay, she had been awestruck by the way Abhay had   grasped his role, delivered his dialogue and acted his part very touchingly. After coming home from the rehearsals, Abhay had shocked both Menon and Neethu by repeating the dialogues of all the actors in the play, without a single mistake. While Menon had just enjoyed his son's uncanny knack to remember the dialogues, it was Neethu, who had appointed Miss. Mitchell to teach Abhay poetry and found appropriate places to showcase his awesome talent.   Menon remembered vividly, seated on a specially designed high chair , how a barely three year old Abhay had enthralled his audience by reciting Mark Anthony's speech and Hamlet's soliloquy. Encouraged by Abhay's instant fame, Neethu concentrated   not only on Abhay's mastering the two tragedies of Shakespeare but also introduced him to Piano, Karate and Western Dance. Naturally, Abhay's days were full with different tutors and coaching.

True, when Abbey's rare talents were widely recognized, Menon too pitched in and prepared his son in whatever way he could, to handle the rare honour and fame. But, very often Menon secretly wondered whether this name and fame was worth curbing the natural tendencies of an innocent five year old.........

'Come on Abhay, why're you so slow in eating your favourite pizza, finish it fast and go to bed early, you need rest". Neethu's shrill voice brought Menon back to the present. He slowly removed his glasses, wiped off its lenses vigorously and looked at his son. He knew only too well that peculiar expression of Abhay, his knitted eyebrows and slightly flaring off his little nostrils, whenever he was hurt. Abhay, like Menon, was very sensitive but unlike the other children of his age ,he was too disciplined, too smart to display his hurt feelings. Menon put his glasses on the paper he was reading, walked towards Abhay and with a sudden clutch of love kissed his forehead and said,

"Abhay, I know you will do very well for the interview tomorrow. Actually it's not even a formal interview; after all, you've faced many interviews extremely well. Isn't it just fun, the TV camera following all your activities, so that the viewers can get a glimpse of what my little son's doing on a Sunday? You don't understand, my son, how great you are now, my little celebrity", Menon laughed. Then shaking Abhay's head gently, he continued, 'you must go to bed early and sleep well so that you would be ready, when the TV crew comes. After that, you will be completely free and you'll have a great vacation of two weeks in Kottayam with Ammomma and Appooppa, we'll bring you many surprise gifts too from New York, Okay? "

Abhay looked up, continued to chew with his mouth tightly shut for a second and then swallowed it before answering, "Okay Dad". Menon stood behind Abhay's chair, till he finished his milk. Once Abhay finished his dinner, Menon accompanied him to his bed room, waited patiently till he brushed his teeth and change into his night pajamas; then Menon put him on his soft bed, wrapped him with his blue comforter and switched off the light. Turning on the bed room lamp, Menon kissed Abhay gently and said in a voice filled with affection,' Good night Abhay , Sleep well , my son'

"Abhay, get a good nights' rest, so that you would be as fresh as a rose for the telecast, Good night sweetie pie'
That was Neethu, planting a hurried kiss on Abhay's forehead.
Though closing his large, luminous eyes, Abhay kissed his Mom and Dad 'Good night'

Abhay tried to sleep but was too excited to sleep, the sweet memories of his last year's stay with his grandparents in 'Kottayam House' kept coming back to his mind. He loved his Ammomma and Appoppa very much, he even loved the way they called him 'Appu' *'Appoooo, what a funny Malayali name to replace Abhay meaning 'fearless'!!'* Mom used say, but Dad was defensive, *'What's wrong with 'Appu' that way, they call me 'Unni' another funny, Malayali name according to you. Abhay loves to be called 'Appu', so what's your problem?'*

Abhay loved not only his grandparents but also their grand, old Kottayam house with its steep tiled roof which had grown dark and mossy with age and rain, doors with not two, but four shutters of paneled teak, antique furniture, huge backyard with guava, tamarind, mango and jackfruit trees. Abhay remembered, Kuttappan was an expert in climbing the trees and it was sheer fun to catch the tiny, thumb-shaped, sour tamarind which Kuttappan plucked and threw from the tamarind tree. Abhay's mouth watered, remembering the taste of brownish-green tamarind with salt. Kuttappan could even climb coconut trees by tying a rope around his feet.

It was hard to believe that Kuttappan, who was slightly taller but much thinner than him, was actually thirteen. Kuttappan said, on all his birthdays, Appooppa gave him his birthday shirt and pants and Ammoomma took him to the temple to do *Puja* in his name. Later she made a great feast with payasam. Appoopa said, Kuttappan was a very clever boy and when he passed his tenth standard, Appooppa would send him to ITI, once he passed his diploma in ITI, he could easily get a job in a big city. Abhay wished he could come to Chennai then.

Abhay liked Kuttappan's small but neat and furniture-less house. Kuttappan's father, told that the house was Ammomma's father's wedding gift to him.. Kuttappan's mother was a great cook, and Abhay enjoyed her *'Kappa and fish curry'*, something which he never tasted before, but it was a 'pinky' secret , as Ammomma said he should not talk about eating that to Mom and Dad.

Abhay's another great attraction was the Kerala monsoon. He loved the sound of raindrops falling on the roof, thunder, croaking of frogs and the sound of crickets on rainy nights. During daytime, it was real fun to sit in the swing-cot and play 'snake and ladder' or 'Trade' with Kuttappan, munching Ammomma's freshly made, hot banana chips and tapioca chips

'Kuttappan's so lucky, no big homework, no tuition, no Piano classes, no stage performances, why, not even School on rainy days because his school roof leaks badly, how funny!!'
Abhay almost muttered aloud and laughed.
Abhay was wide-awake now to relive his happy days in the Kottayam house.

On sunny evenings, Abhay went with Kuttappan for kite flying or fishing. Abhay admired the way Kuttappan squatting on his haunches and threading expertly, coiling, purple earthworms onto hooks on the fishing rod he had made from slender culms of yellow bamboo. Oh! The amazing things Kuttappan could make! He could not only make beautiful, multi-coloured kites but also fly them very, very high. He could also make windmills, balls, snakes, watches and crown with coconut leaves, in a jiffy. And he could draw pictures very nicely and even drew portraits of Abhay, Ammoomma and Appooppa. Abhay was sure that Kuttappan would have been a 'Wonder boy' like

him, if he were in Chennai. On holidays Kuttappan
spent the whole time with Abhay.

Even when Kuttappan had School, Abhay was not
bored because Appooppa took him along for his
morning walks. Holding Appooopppa's hands, Abhay
watched the emerald green paddy fields, gentle swaying
of yam leaves in the breeze, chirping birds, multi
coloured butterflies sucking honey from the wild
growth of hibiscus shrub etc. He remembered vividly ,
how during one morning walk, Appoppa jumped with
joy and kissed him , when he casually recited from the
poem, Miss. Mitchell, had taught him.
"Dull would he be of soul who could pass by a sight so
touching in its majesty'.

Turning his walk into an enjoyable morning-run to keep
up with Appooppa's long strides, Abhay listened in
rapt attention to his adventures at sea , how once his
ship's radar had broken in Bermuda triangle or how in
one winter, his ship had got stuck on ice in Toronto etc.
In Kottayam house Abhay did not sleep alone in a
separate bed room like Chennai There he slept between
Ammomma and Appooppa . After dinner, Appooppa
used to carry Abhay in piggyback to the bedroom,
whenever he protested, *Appoppa, don't carry me, I'm
a big boy now, you would hurt your back'*, Appooppa
would laugh loudly, saying , *'No, Appu, I had carried
your Dad. who was heavier than you at your age, I'm
strong very strong , otherwise how could I be a
Captain of huge ships which carry hundreds of cars
eh?'*

Wrapping his legs around Ammomma's soft, cold
stomach, (*Ammomma, your stomach's as cold as a
fridge'*, he used to say) Abhay heard the stories of the
naughty Lord Krishna, Bhima with his mace and Karna,
the son of Surya, born with gold earrings in his ears and

a gold breast plate on his chest, engraved with the emblem of Sun God etc. Ammomma was a great story-teller and how she used to be choked, when she narrated how Kunti, Karna's mother ,put him in a reed basket and cast him away in a river. On rainy nights, hugging Ammomma tightly Abhay demanded scary stories of Dracula and the Vampires, when Ammomma hesitated , Abhay would say *'Ammomma, you're telling 'No' to your own Appukuttan'* ,that magic sentence always worked and Ammomma would kiss him and narrate very scary stories of Vampires ,who had no shadows, no reflections in the mirror, left no footprints on sand or ripples in water. But those scary stories always ended with a Sanskrit prayer to Lord Hanuman, which he had to repeat after her to prevent getting nightmares.

Reminiscing the fragmented but delightful memories of Kottayam stay, Abhay slowly, but almost unwillingly closed his heavy eyelids and slipped into a sleep………

'Abhay, look, look at that Guava tree, there, there, that ash striped cat's chasing that red, oh, very red chameleon,' holding Abhay's, shoulders, Kuttappan pointed to the Guava tree and said in his excited, squeaky voice .

'Where's it? Where? Where?', asked Abhay impatiently, raising his voice to a high pitch.

'Come on Abhay, you've eyes or buttons? There, there, the third, no no, one… two… three… oh yeah the fourth branch, up there, look, fast', Kuttappan raised his squeaky voice.

'Yeah, I can see, I can see now. Amazing! Amazing!' leaning against Kuttappan, Abhay said, wonder-struck...

'Abhay, you're talking in your dream, come on, son, you've to get ready for the TV', shaking him gently, his Dad said, while a grinning Mom watched…..

Dressed up each time to suit the occasion, Abhay read books, played piano, recited a few verses from Hamlet and Othello, ate food with mom and dad, played computer games, sang, danced and talked casually with the TV person, unmindful of the glaring TV camera following him everywhere. Abhay was very natural, spontaneous and not at all self-conscious. His proud, beaming parents showed thumbs- up signal all the time, to show their approval and immense satisfaction in Abhay's expert handling of the different situations.

'Now, one last and final question Abhay," the TV man was all smiles, 'if you were granted a wish, what would you ask for?', thrusting the mike on Abhay, he asked Abhay thought only for a split second, suddenly all the 'tutored answers ' took a back seat, and the innocent child in him surfaced,
'Well, I would like to be like Kuttappan', Abhay smiled charmingly…

CHASING A SHADOW

Lieutenant Commander Nambiar poured a strong drink, his favorite rum and soda. He deliberately pushed away the unpleasant thought of his recent heart attack and the eminent Cardiologist's strict warning. He knew he was throwing discretion to the winds when he resumed the old habit of drinking and chain-smoking just after a massive heart attack and a month's hospitalization.

"Strictly no drinks and cigarettes, Nambiar," said Dr. Khurana slicing the air with his hands to emphasize his point, "Now that you're transferred to your home -town in Kerala, you've plenty of time to relax. Take long walks, enjoy nature, oh! Plenty of that nature stuff in Cochin, Right?" the friendly Cardiologist laughed and continued, *"Believe me Nambiar, you would be back in Bombay as fit as a fiddle, don't worry."*

Remembering the good Doctor's words, Nambiar smiled nervously.
Dr. Khurana was no doubt an eminent Cardiologist, but how could he ever understand the supreme indifference and total lack of ambition of the once over-ambitious, efficient and most popular helicopter pilot Lt. Commander Nambiar?

True, once Nambiar's life revolved around the impression of Senior Officials, their Confidential Reports and promotions. His ambition knew no limits, "None less than the Chief of Naval Staff—"Admiral Nambiar, doesn't it sound grand, Su?" He used to ask Sudha and silence her initial protests against their tension-ridden, mad, social life. That was long time ago. Now, he was a changed man, nothing to look forward to; a big loser who had lost everything. He had lost his beautiful wife Sudha, who he had loved and married a decade ago. He had lost the love and affection of his nine year old son, who he had bundled off to a renowned Boarding School at the tender age of six. He had lost his health too and already had a heart attack at the young age of thirty-eight. Finally he had lost his career too, after all those covetable assignments, he had to rot as the Commanding Officer of an NCC unit, a post generally meant for the old, superseded Officers. His cup of misery is full to the brim.

Nursing his drink, Nambiar looked around. The multi-colored flowers, the red, yellow, pink and white flowers on the neatly pruned hibiscus bushes, so fresh, bright and beautiful in the morning, now wilted and drooping their petals in a pathetic sort of way as though to share Nambiar's grief..

He looked at his watch and gasped.

"Only 6.30! Time just hangs on here. What a difference from the very busy, mad life I was used to, in Bombay! For that matter, was my entire life in the Navy a race against time? I joined the rat race and forgot to live my life. Can I really blame Sudha for falling a prey to the circumstances, created by me? What a fool I was! By the time I realized that I was chasing a mere shadow, it was too late."

Nambiar wanted to divert his attention from that dangerous zone of thought. He quickly went inside the room and switched on the TV. And alas! the very face he wanted to forget loomed large on it.

Yes, there was Sudha, wrapping a towel which hardly covered her ample bosom, recommending some soap. Nambiar's heart beat violently and he could not help a foolish thrill as he watched the gentle, graceful movements of Sudha's manicured fingers applying soap lather to her beautiful face.

Sudha had not changed a bit, the same shoulder-length hair, the same expressive, twinkling, eyes with long, curved lashes, same smile, even the same way of tilting her head slightly to the left side while talking.....Alas! the flood gate of memories was pushed open again....

Nambiar's mind raced back to that *'Onam'* function, which he had attended with his mother in Town hall.

Saraswathy Amma, the undisputed 'matriarch' of the famous *'Mullakkal'* family and the Correspondent of 'The Nambiar memorial School', which Nambiar's father had founded, was as usual the chief-guest at the *Onam* celebration in the School. As their chauffeur was on leave, Nambiar had to drive his mother to the School, hardly realizing that it was going to be a turning point in his life.

That was the day Nambiar first set eyes on the most beautiful girl he had ever met in his life. Nambiar remembered vividly the way Sudha came to the stage, clad in an off-white, gold border *'mundu* set', the traditional outfit of Nairs'. Her lustrous hair was braided and adorned with lots of jasmine flowers. She had a satin-smooth complexion, large, expressive eyes and aquiline nose, Nambiar noticed even the sexy cleft on her chin. Even the umbrella-shaped ear dangling, the only piece of jewelry she wore, added considerable charm to her oval-shaped face.

While Nambiar was busy registering the perfectly beautiful face on his mind, Sudha walked towards the mike and sang a semi-classical 'Onam' song.

Nambiar was transported to a different world and only the thunderous applause from the audience could bring him back to the present.

That night was a sleepless night for Nambiar. Sudha's beautiful face, her melodious voice, her long, lustrous hair and even the fragrance of the jasmine blossoms on it, haunted him.

From the very next day, Nambiar's gleaming motor bike hovered around Sudha's Women's' College area. He was also quick in finding out the details of the only daughter of a retired School master Raman Nair. Sudha had lost her mother, when she was just a child and she stayed with her grandmother and father in a small house near the Siva temple.

Nambiar followed Sudha for about a fort-night, making his interest very obvious to her. Later, he wrote a letter, expressing his love and honest intention of marrying her, before he left for Bombay to join duty...........

Nambiar suddenly felt very hot. He got up to put on the AC wondering how he started sweating on that December night. He wanted another stiff drink, "*To hell with the Doctor's orders. What's the use of my life, if I can't enjoy even the simple pleasures of living? bullshit*", muttering almost aloud, Nambiar refilled his glass and started slurping his drink....

Nambiar deliberately brought his memory back to his burning desire to possess Sudha. So, when he got Sudha's almost favorable reply subtly hinting the necessity of his meeting her father, he was ecstatic.
The same evening, a triumphant Nambiar reached her College and straight away asked for Sudha Nair, student of Pre-University.

From then on, a debonair Nambiar and his most attractive pillion rider became the most common sight in parks, restaurants, beach and matinee shows and of course the theme of hot gossip.

Finally, with an iron-will Nambiar managed to overcome the tsunami of opposition from his mother and other close relatives, got married to Sudha in Guruvayur Temple and joined duty in Bombay.

After the initial thrill of possessing the most beautiful and talented girl wore off, Nambiar again started concentrating on his Naval career. He was always ambitious and knew pretty well the importance of an active social life in the Navy and the significant role an exquisitely beautiful wife like Sudha could play to further his career.

But, Sudha lacked badly the glamour, sophistication and social skills of other naval wives. Two years' of her College education in a Government College coupled with her shy nature and strict upbringing by an old lady were great impediments. If only she could be groomed to talk English fluently, dress up glamorously, dance well and less inhibited in flaunting her charm, she could contribute tremendously for her husband's achieving his goal.

No doubt, Nambiar was efficient. He even got the President's gold medal in the National Defense Academy. But efficiency alone would not reach him anywhere. He lacked the right pedigree to impress his Senior Officers and influence their confidential reports. He knew only too well the plight of efficient Officers superseded for no fault of their own.

If only he could please his senior Officers! The royal road to a prosperous career lay in transforming Sudha to the most glamorous and sophisticated naval wife. So, a determined Nambiar started concentrating on reforming his charming wife from a sleepy town in Kerala to an ultra-modern Bombayite.

In the beginning, Sudha protested vehemently. She was painfully aware of her limitations; she could not speak English or Hindi, could not dance or mix freely with the Naval crowd .When other Officers commented on her looks, instead of mumbling 'thanks' she blushed and looked down.

Nambiar became severely critical of Sudha's inhibited behavior. After every party, he shouted, "You're only fit to be the wife of some school-master in Kerala. You're a disgrace to me, yes, you are. When're you going to converse and mix freely like other Officers 'wives?"

Sudha wept bitterly; she simply loathed those parties and the hypocrisy around. As though answering her fervent prayers, Mahesh was born which seemed to have subdued Nambiar's vigorous social life considerably. Sudha was happy that Nambiar spent evenings with Mahesh, though frequently with his drinks to celebrate his happiness.

By that time, Lieutenant Commander Nambiar became the Second in Command of a big ship which was the most crucial assignment to reach his goal. And he simply could not afford to displease his Commanding Officer Commander Singh, who with the mere stroke of his pen could mar his career.

Commander Singh was inefficient to the core and a notorious womanizer. But, he was fabulously rich, politically influential and well-connected. He could not only help Nambiar climb the rungs of the promotion ladder but also get him prestigious foreign assignments. As was customary, the Nambiars called on Commander Singh. Welcoming the young couple to his living room, Singh laughed loudly and said, "*Oh*! Lucky man, I'm told the Malabar girls, what's the name", tapping his light blue turban, he paused and then continued '*uh ,uh! Theeya,* yes *Theeya* girls are the prettiest in India, now I'm convinced. Your wife's a beauty," he patted Nambiar's back. Nambiar could not help noticing the wicked gleam and unconcealed admiration in Singh's narrow and close-set eyes when he surveyed the contours of Sudha's voluptuous figure.

Soon, clad in a flowered Punjabi suit Mrs. Singh, a tall, very fair, pleasant-looking lady in her fifties, joined them. But, Sudha could not take part in their lively conversation and had to resort to smiles, nods and occasional monosyllables. Sensing her discomfort, a good-natured Mrs. Singh switched over to Hindi which made Sudha more miserable.

Finally, while taking leave, Commander Singh gave a patronizing, seemingly innocent, tight hug to a visibly embarrassed and annoyed Sudha.

That night, a weeping Sudha tried to convince Nambiar her extreme misery in such social calls and parties, as she could not converse either in English or Hindi. When her plea did not get the desired effect, she vehemently protested against the permissive behavior of his boss. But, much to her chagrin, Nambiar got angry with her and told her that if she wanted him to achieve his goal, she had to be cooperative and understanding.

But after few minutes, with great effort Nambiar controlled his mounting anger and hugged her close and whispered pleadingly in her ear.

"Look Su, you know your face is your fortune and you can do wonders for my, no, no, our future. You met many Officers' wives. Have you seen anyone prettier than you, darling? And how many of them can sing like you? You sing Hindi songs like Lata Mangeshkar but only this good-for-nothing husband of yours can enjoy it; all because you're so inhibited, so shy, so quiet." Then he started kissing her gently whispering to her not-so-reluctant ears, "Darling, I know I'm to be blamed. I still remember you, that beautiful, confidant girl enthralling the crowd with her song on that day, when I first met you. You are still the most charming girl; none of these gossipy wives could hold a candle before you. I'm going to make you shed your inhibitions, just you wait and see."

That Saturday, a completely groomed ultra-modern Sudha with bobbed hair, shaped eyebrows and the most expensive facial, emerged out of Bombay's costliest beauty parlor frequented by film-stars. Nambiar was thrilled to see his wife's incredible metamorphosis.

From then on, there was no looking back. Nambiar spent money lavishly for tutoring and initiating Sudha to the sophisticated Society. He employed a convent-educated, Anglo-Indian lady to coach her to converse in English, that too with an Anglicized accent. He taught her dancing and driving.

Sudha's wardrobe was filled with trendy, glamorous and revealing attires. She lisped English, became an expert in small talk and gossip, picked up   western music by listening to cassettes danced gracefully and effortlessly and even took whisky and soda at parties which inevitably ended with her song.

Nambiar's ambition started soaring higher and higher. "None less than an Admiral Su and you're the wife of the Chief of Naval Staff, Admiral Nambiar, doesn't it sound grand darling?", patting a beaming Sudha , Nambiar chuckled.

Days became weeks, weeks flew into months. The tension-ridden life, the sudden popularity of Sudha, the gossips connecting her with other top brass had not bothered Nambiar.

"Sudha's very popular in the Naval Circle. What if she's a little promiscuous? Who would not be, given her beauty, talents and opportunities? After all, I too had occasional flings with many like Neelima Srivatsa, Neeraja Chopra and Dr. Mukherji, life's short and we've to enjoy every moment of it. Only fools would waste their time on meaningless and idiotic philosophies."

As if to justify his philosophy, Nambiar even kept a framed verse on his writing desk,
"Catch then, Oh! Catch this transient hour,
Improve each moment as it flies
Life is a short summer, man, a flower,
He dies alas! How soon he dies."

The only stumbling block in Nambiars' hectic social life was their son, Kumar. But, soon they bundled him off to an expensive public School. So, life was like a beautiful stream with absolutely nothing to hinder its smooth course.....

"Oh! What a fool I was! I was unreasonably, no, no, insanely ambitious, what happened to my ambition, Chief of Naval Staff, my foot! Rotting in this God-forsaken place, when I'm barely 40. What a terrible mistake!"

Slurping the last drop, Nambiar poured another strong drink, gulped it down and grimaced.

"How I wish death could put an end to my sufferings like my mother and Sudha's Acchamma. Kumar would inherit all my money, Sudha too must be minting money by her modeling. But, with all that money, can Kumar get back his lost childhood or happy home? I deprived my child of a pleasant childhood and a happy family life. How cruel of me! I was blinded by my ambition and destroyed everyone around me and I deserve this punishment."

Nambiar remembered distinctly the previous evening of Sudha's day of crowning glory which ironically turned out to be their Doomsday, when he was called to Singh's cabin.

As soon as he entered the spacious cabin, Commander Singh gave his usual idiotic grin and said, "Do sit sown Nambiar, have a drink with me. What will you have; whisky on rocks, gin and lime or rum and soda?"
"Rum and Soda, Sir", Nambiar smiled.

After about three round of drinks, Singh cleared his throat, dropped his loud voice to a conspiratorial whisper and said, "Nambiar, there's going to be a Beauty Contest, the Navy Queen Contest", tomorrow. And the judges Rahul Singh and Anil Banerjee, both from the film world are my close friends. Why don't you ask Sudha to take part? Sure, she would walk away with the crown; what do you say?"

Nambiar noticed the wicked gleam in Singh's narrow eyes but chose to ignore it. He did not believe in being a possessive, jealous husband and certainly did not mind Sudha's minor flirtations.

"I'll tell her to join the contest, thanks for the drinks, Sir", saluting smartly Nambiar took leave from his boss.

Nambiar remembered Sudha's reaction. She already knew about the contest and was very enthusiastic. She was not a fool to miss a golden chance like that.

Next evening, Nambiar could not take his eyes from his breath-takingly beautiful wife.

Sudha's transparent shocking-pink chiffon saris revealed her hour-glass figure while her sleeveless matching *choli,* her cleavage. An exquisitely designed necklace of precious rubies and pearls adorned her smooth, slender neck. Her long matching ear drops nearly touched her shoulders. Her elaborate hair-do was most suitable for her oval-shaped face. Everything about her was simply fascinating, sparkling eyes, perfect nose, full lips, dimpled chin. Sudha always reminded Nambiar of Thomas Hardy's description of 'Tess". Like Tess, in Sudha's case too, despite her full figure, phases of her childhood still lurked from her flawless complexion, innocent eyes, sweet curve of her upper lip and even from the cleft on her chin.

When the Nambiars reached the banquet hall of the Naval Mess, admiring glances followed Sudha. Sudha was conscious of the stunning effect of her presence on the audience and waved at them charmingly.

Finally, a supremely confident Sudha paraded, gracefully and effortlessly on the stage. She was certainly the most beautiful girl among the bevy of beauties. Nobody was surprised, when the panel of judges unanimously selected Sudha Nambiar as the 'Navy Queen'.

Amidst the loud cheering and thunderous applause of an enthusiastic crowd, the Admiral crowned the 'Navy Queen'…

Sudha danced with the Admiral, Senior Officers and distinguished film stars. An uninhibited Sudha mixed freely with the admiring crowd, giggled at all their silly jokes and carried on conversation effortlessly. Holding her very close to him, Singh too danced, when Nambiar looked on helplessly.......

Nambiar should have been the happiest man because this was the day he had been dreaming of, all these years. His efforts were amply rewarded. His once shy, coy, beautiful bride from a sleepy town in Kerala was transformed to a breathtakingly beautiful and most sophisticated 'Navy Queen'. A great achievement indeed!

But, somehow Nambiar felt unhappy, in fact felt miserable. He felt a nagging pain surging inside, gradually developing and engulfing his whole being in its terrible grip. He felt a strange and inexplicable suffocation. He mentally compared the glamorous 'Navy Queen' with the simple, modest and charming Sudha he met a decade ago.

Sudha had come a long way from there. No, he had dragged her along. But, now he felt strangely insecure. None could stop her now. Was his ambition infectious? Sudha had run the marathon with him and somewhere along she had lost her innocence, child-like simplicity and modesty. Sudha did not belong to Nambiar alone anymore and obviously she seemed to love and enjoy the glare of publicity.

Suddenly, the band stopped playing and a dazed Nambiar was led to the dinner table. Many congratulated the Navy Queen's 'lucky' husband, praised him to the skies. But behind those flattering comments, a hardly- sober Nambiar suspected a veneer of contempt for him, the helpless husband of a renowned beauty.

During the hour-long drive home, Nambiar was quiet, hardly listened to Sudha's incessant chatting. All he wanted was to reach home, pick up a fight with her and throw her out of his house and life…

Once they reached the bed room, in a voice quivering with anger, Nambiar asked, "What happened to you? Were you drunk? You were openly, shamelessly flirting with all those idiots and reveling in their attention. It's time you stopped all your flirting, I gave you a long rope, it's my mistake. Sure, you haven't forgotten your miserable, poverty-stricken existence as the daughter of a School master in some village? Any one in my shoes would've shot you right away."
Showing his mounting fury through his clenched teeth, Nambiar walked towards his wife menacingly, grabbed her shoulders and shook violently.

Pushing him away, Sudha laughed, "*Ha Ha!* How wonderful to know that my husband is a 'Forgiving angel'! But, this hurt-husband role does not suit the future Naval Chief of Staff, Admiral Nambiar"

The unmistakable sarcasm in Sudha's tone infuriated Nambiar further and he pushed her with all his strength to the wall, started hitting her mercilessly till she lost her balance and fell on the floor. Panting like an animal, Nambiar left the room…..

The next morning, Nambiar got up very late only to learn that Sudha had already left the place.

When Sudha's divorce petition came, Nambiar had to give in, after a futile attempt for a compromise. By the time the divorce came through, Sudha had already established as the most well-paid, sought-after model in Bombay....

Excessive drinking and chaotic life – style had taken its heavy toll on Nambiar and resulted in his first, massive heart-attack and subsequent transfer to Kerala after Medical categorization......

Nambiar looked at his watch and gasped, the late night Malayalam serial was on the TV. There again the advertisement of Sudha soaping her beautiful, slender neck and bare shoulders, "The secret of my beauty......." Her melodious voice filled the air....

Nambiar tried to get up but sat down as the entire room was reeling before him. He saw Sudha clearly with her ankle length, lustrous, braided hair and the jasmine blossoms entwined on it. He could feel the fragrance of her sandalwood soap mingled with the jasmine blossoms.

"Su, come closer, let me hold you; I'm sorry, terribly sorry darling. I love you, I love Kumar. I'll bring Kumar back from the boarding school. Let's live happily, just the three of us; let's forget the past, forget the Navy, forget everything and start life afresh.

Su, sing that *Onam* song which had brought us together, *huh!* I'm enjoying, what a melodious voice!

Hold me, hold me tight, my heart's beating violently like that 'drum' on that *Onam* day, Can't you see how happy I'm, let's celebrate our reunion.".........

The next morning, the hotel boy ,who brought Nambiar his breakfast saw him slumped in a chair very close to the TV and the set was still on.......

Newspapers carried the obituary with Nambiar's picture in Naval Uniform, below it was written,

'Lt. Commander Nambiar passed away, following a massive heart attack in a hotel room. He is survived by his only son, Kumar.'

CHANGE OF HEART

Vandana did not mind the hour-long wait at the medical college stop although her friends Radhika and Neelima started grumbling. In fact, Vandana enjoyed standing at the crowded bus stop waiting for bus as she could almost feel the admiring glances of the passersby. Further bus travels are a rare experience for her, not that she had never travelled by bus. She used to travel only bus once upon a time. But that was a long time ago, nearly a decade ago, when she was barely eight.

Things were different then. Her father Rama Rao was only a petty officer in the Indian Navy. But Dame Luck really smiled at him when he voluntarily retired from the Navy and joined a foreign liner and made enough money, though it meant a lot of separation from his wife and two children. Prema, Rama Rao's wife, did not seem to mind her husband's absence as long as she could live in a posh bungalow, go around in a chauffeur driven-car, flaunting her wealth through her chunky gold jewelry and costly saris. One by one all the other status symbols followed - Presidentship of ladies club, membership in voluntary organizations which was instrumental in getting publicity of her social service, etc., etc. Often she told her friends, "My Vandana brought us luck. She has an excellent horoscope. It predicted that she would be very wealthy one day. That's why we named her "Sreelakshmi", Goddess of wealth. You know, her real name is Sreelakshmi though we call her Vandana at home."
She went on and on in one breath, the minutest details of their collection of jewelry, investments, shares, etc. etc.

Prema knew that she was an object of envy among her neighbors and enjoyed her "Superior" status. She had completely forgotten her past. If Prema could forget the days she stood in the queue at ration shops and crowded bus stop in addition to the monotonous routine of cooking, washing, feeding and taking children to far-off, lesser-known schools without any assistance from even a part time Ayah, Vandana's short memory was not only pardonable, but also natural and expected. After all, she was sweet seventeen. What was more, she was at the top of the world when Rs. Twenty lakhs doled out as capitation fee, could get her the coveted medical seat, while many of her friends with very high marks could not even dream of getting into medical college.

Vandana not only resembled her mother in looks with the black long curly hair, flawless wheatish complexion, bright eyes and slightly upturned nose, but also in her general outlook. Just like Prema enjoyed exhibiting every piece of her jewelry, her innumerable imported gadgets to all her club members and friends, Vandana too enjoyed being the center of attraction in her college with her fabulous collection of saris, churidar sets and matching accessories, carefully collected from all over the world by her loving father.

Vandana thanked her stars that her driver had gone on a week's leave to his village, as it gave her more chances of exhibiting herself with her newly – acquired medical coat on her right shoulder during her bus journeys.

Vandana adjusted her turquoise chiffon sari and gently patted her right shoulder again and again, a mannerism she had acquired in her two weeks' stay in the medical college. She loved that feeling when her carefully manicured fingers touched the smoothness of the soft white coat.

Vandana could not help smiling, when she thought of the sensation she created among the senior medical students. She got "ragged" every day. She was surrounded by a gang of seniors who, demanded her to sing, dance, imitate her favorite star etc. They shot questions, commented about her looks and refined taste in dressing. She enjoyed being the center of attraction and knew only too well that ragging was only a compliment in disguise as most of the plain looking Janes were left alone. She could not help smiling when she thought of Harish's repeated comments that she strongly resembled Catherine Zeta Jones.

Suddenly Radhika's voice woke her up from her day dreaming. "Hey, where are you Sreelakshmi? Still thinking of Harish? He seems to have quite a crush on you." Neelima added hastily, "Quite true, you should have seen his pathetic face when you did not turn up yesterday. Poor thing, he came to me and enquired about you in as casual a tone as possible, but I could sense his disappointment and anxiety. I really pitied him then," Vandana giggled, obviously pleased with her friends' remarks and said, "Well, he offered me a lift, but I refused. I want to act little tough. Later perhaps..." Before she could finish her sentence, the crowded bus to Patel Nagar reached the stop. Vandana and her friends pushed their way into the bus and occupied the vacant seats quickly.

Vandana took the change and demanded three tickets to Patel Nagar. After getting the tickets she surveyed her fellow passengers. The bus was as usual, over-crowded. There were two or three rows of standing passengers, both men and women hanging on to the iron bar above their heads. Many men, most of them youngsters, were on the steps of the entrance. She was amazed to notice that many of them had hardly a foot on the foot-board and clung to the side bar of the bus. The bus seemed to be spilling with people. She wondered where this sea of humanity was going and why everyone seemed to be in a great hurry.

Vandana ran her fingers up and down her white coat again and leaned against her seat near the window. She wanted her friends to continue their chat on Harish. She liked him. He was not strikingly handsome, but he was fair, tall with a mop of unmanageable brown thick hair which matched his bright brown eyes and bushy eyebrows. His booming voice and loud laughter showing his fine teeth, sent waves of excitement on her. *'Something really magnetic about his personality. He has an indescribable charm when he smiles. When he laughs his face looks as innocent as a small kid's'* thought Vandana. Aloud, she said, "Harish is handsome, isn't' he? He has a terrific dress sense. Nothing escapes his scrutinizing eyes. How he notices my dress and comments on them!!"

"He's a great orator and won last year's "Talk your way to the U.S.A contest" of Air India. He's an extremely talented actor and a good mimic too. There was a write-up on him in 'the Hindu'; you are really lucky Sreelakshmi. Some people have all the luck in this world", Radhika added, heaving a deep sigh.

Vandana laughed loudly showing her pearly teeth. She could already feel the admiring eyes of almost everyone around on her and as usual she enjoyed it.

Vandana looked around and her eyes fell on Auntie Kalyani. She was shocked for a moment. Yes, that was unmistakably Auntie Kalyani, who was her neighbor in 'Nehru Nagar'. Kalyani looked horribly old. She must be close to seventy now. She was staying all alone in the small flat adjacent to Vandana's, as she was an old spinster. She remembered the mouth-watering sweets Auntie Kalyani used to make for *"Murugan Sweet Home"*, where she was employed.

Flashing across Vandana's mind were innumerable pictures of the old lady squatting on the floor busy with her never ending process of making *'murukkus'*, *'cheedais'* and sweets on the stove, wiping in between the sweat with a towel, carrying her brother Kishore, letting him help himself with as much *murukku* or *cheedai* as he could eat, assisting her mother on all festival days, taking them to all the nearby temple for listening to a music concert or witnessing the dance performance etc. etc.

Now Auntie Kalyani looked very old and haggard. There she was standing, clutching her old worn-out bag on one hand while her free hand holding on to the iron bar and struggling to balance. Vandana could not help pitying the old pathetic figure standing there, but she was in no mood to acknowledge the old lady's friendship and leave her seat. She certainly did not want to be reminded of her one-room house and the poverty-stricken existence there, when she had envied the rich with fashionable frocks and dresses going to schools in cars.

That was a thing of the past. Now, people envied her, what if her Appa had to 'float' for providing these luxuries. Money is money and it could buy her everything, including a seat in the medical college, which would be an added attraction in the "marriage-market'. Her Appa could buy Harish or anyone else she selected. So, when her life seemed to be 'Roses' all the way, she did not want a painful reminder of her sad past. Further, she had to leave her seat for the old lady and stand there perhaps answering the endless questions from such an unimpressive lady.

So, Vandana quickly decided to pretend that she was a total stranger to her. She could see from the corner of her eye that Kalyani was looking at her. But, she was almost sure that the old woman would not be able to recognize her. Even those days she had cataract and wore thick glasses and now her eye-sight must be worse. Further, how could she associate the glamorous, medical college student with the once extremely thin girl in tight pony tail?

Vandana cleverly avoided Kalyani's glances and continued her chat with her friends, ignoring the old woman completely. She was glad that none of her friends really knew her pet name 'Vandana'. Even if the old woman called her by name, she could pretend that she was not Vandana, so she sat confidently.

Kalyani somehow managed to come near and gently tapped on her shoulder and asked her "Aren't you Vandana? Forgotten your auntie, eh? You are grown so much. How's Kishore? He was my pet. How's your Amma? I don't even know where exactly you are put up? Otherwise I would have come to meet you all and '...she paused for a moment and then continued, 'you know it's not like those days. Now, I'm very weak and don't make *murukkus and cheedais* daily. Only once a month I work, remember the way I used to labor hours together and make snacks and sweets for that 'sweet home?' Why should I work so much, after all? For whom? I'm satisfied with butter milk and rice twice a day. Tell me about yourself. I'm so happy to see you so grown, so pretty. How time flies!"
The old lady would have continued her talk, had she not been struck by the complete blank expression on Vandana's face.

Vandana cleared her throat and said firmly in a cold matter-of-fact tone, "I am not Vandana. I don't know who you are referring to. I'm sorry," and she looked away. Her friends giggled, young men standing along with the old lady burst into laughter; someone among them remarked loudly, "Look at the cunning old woman. Now-a-days these old people are very smart. This old lady thought that she could snatch the seat from that girl pretending friendship, poor thing, sadly disappointed". Most of the passengers, bored with a long journey in the crowded bus, enjoyed immensely the joke at the expense of the old lady and laughed heartily. Radhika and Neelima thoroughly enjoyed the scene and laughed loudly. Vandana too tried to laugh but she felt very uncomfortable. She could carry on the conversation only with great effort. Her mind wandered. She watched the old lady standing there, a picture of supreme misery. She was struggling to stand there. Every jerk of the bus seemed to throw her off her balance. Vandana felt sorry. But then it was too late. The damage was already done to the old lady, who was so loving and affectionate to her entire family.

"Did she really recognize me? Could she see through my motive?" Her mind pondered over these questions over and over again. She felt miserable and restless in her seat. She was ashamed of her callous behavior. She wished "Nehru Nagar" could come quickly....

At last the bus screeched into a halt at Nehru Nagar, three stops ahead of Vandana's and the old lady got down. She pushed her way through the crowd and came outside and stood near the window where Vandana was seated. Raising her voice with a great effort to make it audible to Vandana, she said "Please convey my love and blessings to Kishore. He must be a big boy now. My love to Prema too. All the best my child" and walked away, clutching her bag containing a bunch of spinach among other things. Vandana looked and was relieved to note that neither her friends nor anyone else noticed this, as people were busy getting in and out of the bus. Further Kalyani's feeble voice was almost drowned in the noise outside.

Somehow suddenly others did not seem to matter to Vandana anymore. Auntie Kalyani's face, full of crisscross lines that "wounded animal" look in those small eyes hidden behind thick glasses, her thin fragile frame in the traditionally worn nine yards faded blue sari, haunted Vandana. She felt miserable.

'Oh God, what have I done? How could I insult such a noble lady?' How could I stoop so low? Very mean and cruel of me. How very noble of her to take leave from a girl who, humiliated her in front of so many people? She loved Kishore, she loved me and my mother and she meant what she said'. All of a sudden Vandana remembered how Auntie Kalyani spent sleepless nights, taking charge of their entire household chores, giving her mother courage and comfort, when both Kishore and she were down with measles. Auntie Kalyani was the pillar on which her mother leaned against, then.

Vandana was suddenly filled with a loathing for her mother's meaningless 'social service'. *'How could my mother, the 'renowned 'social worker discard such a noble friendship? How could she be so ungrateful just because she became rich? I couldn't have behaved better. Like mother, like daughter. My mother never really taught me the real values in life. Her life centered on showing off her newly acquired wealth. 'Social Service' my foot! If Appa were here, things might have been different'.*

Vandana's mind was clouded with confusing thoughts. Auntie Kalyani, who belonged to the so-called lower strata of society, taught her a lesson on human kindness. Vandana was moved to tears. She could feel a strange awakening in her soul. She could not ignore that 'inner voice' reprimanding and condemning her for her unpardonable, callous behavior towards someone, who was overflowing with the milk of human kindness.

'My true repentance would move her. Perhaps my behavior, along with the other youngsters' who had fun at the old lady's expense, is the folly of the youth. But, what's the use of all our education, if we can't conduct, if we are devoid of all noble feelings like compassion and love for our fellow beings, respect for elders, etc.? Surely this is a 'wounded civilization' we are all primitive and our sophistication is only a coating. T.S. Elliott perhaps means people like us, when he wrote.
    "We are the hollow men,
    We are the stuffed men,
    Leaning together, head
    Piece filled with straw"
    How much more civilized and cultured Auntie Kalyani is compared to us, 'the hollow' and the 'stuffed'? I'm worse than Judas who betrayed Jesus. But as Jesus said, true repentance would wash away all sins. Yes it was 'sin' to be ungrateful and my repentance only could wash away that sin. It's time I turned a new leaf.'

Vandana was lost in thought and she did not know when the bus reached her stop. Her friend's words "Get down Sreelakshmi, what happened to you," brought her back to the present. She got down mechanically and walked along with her friends, till she found an auto rickshaw slowing down in front of them. Quickly, she hopped into it and said. "Take me to Nehru Nagar, Low Income Group flats, 10th Cross

Lane". Before the auto started, she craned her head out and told her bewildered friends. "I am going to Auntie Kalyani's house. Remember, the old lady whom I disowned in the bus? She was my family friend and neighbor long ago, when I was poor. I'm actually Vandana, Yes, that's what they call me at home"

TRUTH OF THE HEREAFTER

Raman Nair was awake now, the effect of drugs slowly wearing off. Again, the noise of the creaking fan... He stared at the ceiling and the yellow light which attracted innumerable insects.

"Why is it   these insects are so fascinated by the light? Yes, life is like that yellow bright light, and I am like one of these insects desperately trying to cling to it. How I wish I can live a few more years!"

Raman Nair smiled a nervous smile. He looked around as if trying to divert his thoughts, but again the same familiar hospital surroundings, the pungent smell of dettol, nurses in their heavily starched white uniforms, doctors with their white coats and stethoscopes around their necks, Patients in stretcher......

"Oh God, no escape from all this. I am doomed. What a punishment for me, who enjoyed always robust health! How I loathe these hospitals! Now, I will not see my home again".

Ah, the pain was coming back again, slowly. What an injustice! Wasn't Raman Nair a good soul always? Hadn't he spent half of his life on pilgrimages and fasts, to please his favorite deity, *'Ayyapan'.* He had been to *Sabarimalai* eighteen continuous years, and even planted a coconut tree there. He had donated much to charity. What if it was to escape income-tax and for the pleasure of seeing his name in print in leading dailies? Money was money and his generosity did help the poor and needy. He was regular in breaking coconuts at the nearby Ganesh Temple and always prayed for longevity and for death, inevitable as it was, to be quick, painless and peaceful when it came. But now, at the age of 55, he lay like a vegetable with all his hopes shattered....

How handsome and dignified he was with his tall figure and thick-framed glasses and irresistible charm, till recently. Now, it all seemed years ago, though only a month had passed in this wretched hospital. How cruel God could be!

Raman Nair closed his eyes, surprised at his own ingratitude to 'Ayyappan'. 'Saranam Ayyappa' he muttered. After all, hadn't he reached the top of the ladder of success from a humble beginning? Didn't he own a palatial house, an array of servants, marry off his daughter Shalini to a businessman's engineer son? Wasn't he proud of his son, Dr. Shabari (named after his favorite deity again), who was the head of the Department of Economics at Bombay University? Oh, yes he had been lucky. But, still, he was not ready to leave this beautiful world.

The thought of death brought him memories of his wife Lakshmi, whom death had snatched away at the prime of his glory.
'If only my Lakshmi were alive! Ayyappa why didn't you grant me the privilege of being looked after by my loving, devoted and uncomplaining wife?'

Raman Nair remembered bitterly how he ignored her and how she never complained, in spite of her awareness of his roving eye. Though she knew of his innumerable affairs with pretty women, she never troubled him about details. She was happy, contented looking after her two children and house. She was lucky; she lived enough to see her children settled. Had she been alive, she wouldn't have been able to put up with the 'other woman' in her life – Archana, the beautiful Bengali wife of her only son, Dr. Shabari.

Raman Nair drifted away to his life in his son's house in Bombay. How he was ignored, ridiculed and bullied by his sophisticated daughter-in-law! He was an embarrassment to their social activities, parties and intellectual discussions. Raman Nair remembered the final showdown and his son's harsh words, which made him come way to his ancestral home in Kerala and the terrible loneliness till cancer brought him back to a Bombay hospital.

The heavy footsteps on the staircase... The Doctor was coming. Raman Nair closed his eyes-Cigarette fumes filled the room. Doctor examined him with his usual pinned-on smile, and patted him reassuringly and went away. *'The hypocrite!'* murmured Raman Nair. *'Who is he trying to fool with his encouraging smile? Don't I know that my days are numbered?'*

Suddenly voices outside. Raman Nair tried to concentrate. Doctor was discussing him with Shabari, his daughter Shalini and son-in-law, who had arrived a week ago. He could hear their discussions. What was it that Shalini pleading in between sobs? He had an urge to ask and console his beloved, loyal daughter. But he controlled himself, realizing that his voice was hardly audible even when someone was nearby. Now he could hear his son's protesting voice.

"Don't be silly, Shalini. What's the use of taking father all the way to New York? It is a sheer waste of money. There is no cure ultimately for this cancer."

"Oh, don't be ungrateful. Didn't father earn enough money? Remember, your present fortune is due to his hard work. How I remember his driving miles to get you, your favorite pastries from a far off bakery, when you were a boy. The moment you demanded a motorbike just to show off, when you were just a student, he got you that. Oh God, 'how he loved us!"

Shabari's voice rose to a high pitch now — "Who said he was not a good father? Am I neglecting him? Didn't I bring him to this hospital when he complained of pain? I gave him all comforts in my house. But he was adamant and stuck up. Was it my fault that he went away to Kerala, I'm only trying to be practical?"

It was Rajan's, Shalini's husband's turn to talk. He said in a soft but firm voice, "Don't behave like an illiterate, Shalini. Shabari is right. Taking him to New York is a sheer waste of money."

That firmly settled the discussion and Raman Nair wished he were deaf.

Shalini came into the room with a tear-stained face and kissed Raman Nair. He said in his feeble voice. "Don't cry for me, darling. Everything is in *Ayyappa's* hands, and we will have to obey His Will - I will be alright soon. Go and take rest. I must sleep now". He kissed her gently, controlling his strong urge to cry.

Raman Nair looked at the yellow light; most of the insects clinging to it had fallen down, dead. He smiled nervously noticing the striking similarity of his case. Now he imagined his death. Sure, Shalini would feel terrible. She was such an affectionate and loving daughter always. But soon, tears would dry on her cheeks. Her husband and children would drag her back to life.

Raman Nair could imagine the condolences, one minute silence and resolution in Dr. Shabari's university.

Newspapers would certainly write an obituary not forgetting to mention Dr. Shabari's achievements and the recent award of his brilliant paper on 'World Economy'. He could imagine Shabari performing the final rites too. After some days, Shabari would pick up the little souvenirs of his bones and ashes from his pyre to deposit in Benares so that Raman Nair would get a permanent place in heaven.....

"That will do, that will do, let me die quickly. If only I were not so much in love with life, which finally let me down. Saranam Ayyappa", Raman Nair muttered almost aloud.

'TILL DEATH DO US PART'

Sipping whisky on rocks from the posh bar of the executive launch of Heathrow airport, Captain John looked around. Except for an old couple in a remote corner and a distinguishing looking man in Savile suit on the sofa opposite, the place was empty. He had to spend four long hours before he could board his flight to Chennai. Under normal circumstances, he would not have ignored the 'let's get acquainted' look on the VIP's eyes. He only knew too well that he never failed to impress his listeners with his adventurous experiences laced with humorous anecdotes in the unfathomable sea as a captain for three decades.

But now he was in no mood to start a conversation with any stranger. At last he was glad that he said 'sayonara' to his sea career, to follow his heart's desire of settling down in his home-town in Kerala, surrounded by singing streams, emerald green paddy fields, coconut grove, wild growth of hibiscus in different colors. He was so excited that he was going to that beautiful place to reconstruct his as well as his son Ashwin's lives; yes, for the first time he was going to have a family, a real home with a loving and devoted wife, a mother to his son Ashwin.

Captain John wondered how his rich and sophisticated friends with their Gymkhana culture, would react to the news of his third marriage in his late fifties ,to a simple, ordinary-looking, middle class, school teacher. He could very well imagine the jokes at his expense, the laughter, the cynical remarks and the endless gossip comparing Sarah with his ex-wives. But, that did not matter to him as he did not intend to belong to that hypocritical, partying, sophisticated upper class society anymore.

True, John wasted the major part of his life in the endless pursuit of fame, fortune and success. Of course he made enough money and was always a resourceful and successful Captain. But, could all that money accumulated over the years, buy him his lost youth and Ashwin his lost childhood? At least now, he should think of his son's and his future and happiness. Others did not matter to him any longer and he had no time to waste keeping up appearances.

"Wisdom of the old, but do they really grow wise with age? Was it lack of wisdom or far-sightedness which doomed my two marriages? Or was it just fate? My life would have run a different course, had I not met Rini. How strange! She could destroy me not one but twice successfully. But with all her incredible beauty, is she really a woman?
"Isn't she a Vampire who could destroy everyone who comes into contact with her? At least, to some extent I'm responsible for my agonizing experiences. But what has Ashwin done to go through a deprived childhood in a Boarding School? Coming to think of it, I do deserve this punishment for falling a prey to Rini's irresistible charm."

Forgotten years enveloped John again. Activated by a peg of whisky, memories gushed through his tired brain. He remembered vividly the cursed day of his life, the day he first set eyes on Rini at a party hosted by his uncle Captain Mathews on board his ship 'Aditya Prabha'. Captain Mathews was always very proud of his nephew's gift of the gab and knew that the young Captain's presence in the party would make it a grand success.

John was not strikingly handsome, but he was athletic, fair with light brown eyes, his thick, curly hair brushed back in typical malayali style. He laughed easily and could carry on an intelligent, interesting and humorous conversation with any age group.

Dressed in an impeccable ash gray suit, John reached the ship a little late for the party. Muttering apologies for his late arrival, he turned around and then his eyes fell on a girl, who just then entered the gangway escorted by a young cadet. For an electrifying moment, John's heart stood still. Draped in sequined turquoise blue chiffon sari with matching accessories, she was breathtakingly beautiful.

Not only John but all the other guests also turned to look at the beautiful lady. Sensing the urgency of answering their unasked question, Captain Mathews said loudly, "Hi Rini, welcome aboard, really honored to have the most beautiful girl for the party" and gently led her to where John was standing. "Johnny, meet Rini, Rini Simon, sure, you must've read about Rini's divorce in all the leading dailies. Rini, this's John, my nephew, Johnny, you better unfold yourself; "I've to look after my other guests."

For the first time in his life, John was tongue–tied. He wanted time to recover from the shock of coming face to face with Rini, who had risen to the status of a celebrity due to her obtaining divorce from Simon, on the ground of impotency at a time when divorce was unheard of among the Syrian Christians of Kerala. Though John read every word of the sensational and interesting 'Rini Divorce Case', he never, not even in his wildest imagination, thought Rini to be such a beauty.

To get over his initial nervousness, he quickly gulped down his whisky and disappeared to fix a 'bloody mary' for Rini. While passing bloody Mary to Rini, his fingers felt the smoothness of Rini's carefully manicured fingers. John stared at Rini unashamedly.

Rini had a glowing complexion. And her eyes were of transparent light gray with contrasting, unusually curved black eye lashes. She had a straight nose and John noticed even the black mole on her sweetly curved upper lip. She smiled a great deal and when she smiled, her dimples showed.

Slowly, conversation flowed like the liquor flowed from the uniformed stewards' hands. Suddenly, stroking her silky, shoulder-length hair, ruffled by the sea breeze, Rini cooed, "Johnny, you forgot to tell me what you do for a living."

Not wasting an opportunity to impress Rini, John quoted Coleridge,
"Alone, alone, all, all alone
Alone in a wide, wide sea
Not a saint took pity on,
My soul in agony."

And continued looking at the eyes of the most beautiful woman he met, "Well, this time, when I sail, instead of my soul in agony, it would be 'my soul in ecstasy' if you so desire Rini, everything depends on your decision, yes, I love you."

Looking back, John did not know how he had said that to Rini, a total stranger. Was it Dutch courage? Or his desperate need to be in love or his over-anxiety to possess the incredibly charming woman, he was not sure. All he remembered now was the tornado created by his decision to marry a divorcee, his grief-stricken mother, warnings of Uncle Mathews and endless arguments of friends and well-wishers. They all said that Rini was solely responsible for Simon's suicide due to his extremely humiliating experiences during trial.

John remembered distinctly his mother's pathetic face when she had pleaded with him not to trust Rini, who must have lied to get that divorce. But, he was under Rini's spell and could easily ignore the valid arguments and gloomy predictions as the result of their burning jealousy. In fact, he imagined that he had risen to the rank of a 'hero' by marrying a divorcee, defying all social conventions.

Rini initially sailed around the world with John, collected exquisite Swarovski crystal and murano glass accessories, exotically designed dresses like 'flamenco' dress etc. which increased her charm tenfold. Her life revolved around pleasure, fun and the admiration of everyone around her. She could love none but herself. She loathed being a mother as she believed that motherhood would destroy her dream figure and diminish her charm considerably.

John attributed Rini's attention-seeking method due to her narcissistic tendency and the solution was a baby, who would make her more mature and divert her attention from herself.

'What a horrible mistake it was! If Ashwin were not born, she would not have continued to be my wife for ten long years. How could I possibly know Rini's innumerable affairs, when she played the role of a loving wife and devoted mother rather well, during my occasional visits? Rini's role as a Receptionist in a five star Hotel was like a web and of course she got entangled in that web of fun, pleasure, sex and scandal. As was always the case, I was the last one to hear the

scandals connecting my wife with that rich business man, that too a happily married man with two sons.'

John remembered the utter callousness in which Rini made her final exit.

As usual, loaded with presents for Rini and Ashwin, John reached Chennai. He did not announce his arrival as he wanted to spring a surprise on them. But, it was John, who was surprised, nay, shocked when his frantic calls to Rini, soon after berthing his ship in Chennai harbor, were not answered. What happened to Rini? Was Ashwin seriously sick? When his desperate attempts to contact Rini failed, a panic-stricken John woke up their neighbor Captain Bali in the middle of the night.

John could never forget that sympathetic tone in Bali's voice, when he reassured them that Ashwin was in a Boarding School since a month, as Rini had left the country, leaving a letter and key of their apartment for John on arrival.

The rest was like a horrible nightmare, so sudden, so unexpected and so unbelievably cruel that he hated to relive except for once, just once to narrate to Sarah.

Slurping the last drop of whisky, John remembered that Rini's letter... no note, had only one sentence. *'Wish there's an easier way to break the news that I'm no longer your wife!'* So brief, so melodramatic and so hurting. It was Captain Bali ,who narrated the sequence of events, Rini's stormy love affair with the well-known Industrialist Koshy Varghese , a much –married man and her final disappearance with him.

John's first impulse was to chase Rini and kill her but he knew he was helpless as none had a clue about

Rini's whereabouts. But, the urge to take revenge was so strong that he managed to trace the address of the deserted wife in Ernakulum....

Suddenly, the announcement of the arrival of some new flights woke John from his reverie. While replenishing his drink, John noticed the lounge getting crowded. But that did not stop him from continuing his chain of thought.

John remembered the atmosphere in the Cochin Naval Mess where he met Alice, was very much similar to the lounge, except for the soft music flowing from the stereo and the uniformed bearers serving drinks and dinner to the customers, almost interrupting their animated talk. Unfamiliar with such a scenario, Alice was visibly nervous and uncomfortable.

In the dim light, John could not see Alice very clearly but, he guessed she was in her forties. Though fair-complexioned, she was on the fat side, had a round face, beady eyes and blunt nose. John could not help noticing the draperies of white flesh hanging whenever she lifted her arms. She was absolutely the antithesis of the incredibly attractive, suave and glamorous Rini.

John could almost understand Alice's husband falling a prey to Rini's irresistible charm but how could he possibly desert his wife and two children so cruelly? John could not help admiring the helpless woman's tremendous love and affection for her sons. And he heard with dismay, how Alice's parents had paid a huge dowry for her worthless husband and how he had been a loving husband and doting father to their 10 and 8 year old sons, till Rini had entered his life six months ago. In that two hours' narration, Alice did not express her hatred towards her husband; on the contrary Rini was the object of her intense hatred.

At the end of the meeting, John was sure that it was Rini, who was solely responsible for breaking Alice's happy home. When John dropped Alice home, he met Sajiv and Sujit, her sons and liked them instantly.

Soon, without realizing the implications, John was playing the father-figure for the two boys, Ashwin too got along marvelously with Sajiv, Sujit and Auntie Alice, whenever he was on vacation.

After a couple of months, John found himself caught in a labyrinth of totally unexpected emotions. Revenge on Rini had been slowly replaced by love, affection and compassion for the unfortunate Alice, who could love Ashwin as her own son. Soon, John started imagining the possibility of a new life ,a new home for all of them and suggested Alice moving with her sons to his posh bungalow in Chennai.

Once again, deviating from all social norms, John took Alice and children to Chennai. With great difficulty, he also got admission for the three boys in a renowned School in Chennai. John was all admiration for Alice's tremendous sense of adaptability and her supreme efforts to suit the society which fate had placed her. She frequented beauty parlors, bobbed her long hair, shaped her eyebrows, dressed up in modern outfits and looked very sophisticated. She talked English, became an expert in small talk and learnt driving. Alice's new found confidence was so amazing that John felt extremely proud of her metamorphosis.

Once their divorces came through John and Alice became man and wife. His friends congratulated him and laughed heartily at his humorous comment quoting Samuel Johnson, "Triumph of hope over experience."

Captain John sighed deeply and looked at his watch. Only an hour passed since his mind raced back and forth covering a span of more than a decade. He deliberately brought his mind back to the day, when his eyes were opened to reality.

John had to stay in Japan for a year, supervising the building of a new ship and bringing her to Tuticorin in her maiden voyage. From Tuticorin, an ecstatic John reached his house in Chennai by a hired van which carried three exquisitely designed study tables from Japan for the boys. John knew Alice's weakness for rare pieces of jewelry with precious stones.. She already had opal from Sydney, diamonds from Antwerp, corals from Italy and Murano jewelry from Venice. So, this time John wanted to surprise her with Micki-motto pearls from Japan.

When John reached home, he was shocked to see Alice, an unrecognizably slim Alice, sporting a shirt and jeans, not only looking years younger but also very pretty. What happened to her fat arms, pot belly and clumsy figure? He always thought, though never mentioned that her bobbed hair and modern outfits did not suit her matronly look. Now, how could she achieve this miracle?

Concealing his initial shock, John said, "Alice, you've lost a lot of weight and look so charming. Can't wait to hear the secret of my wife's dream figure. Where are the boys; as usual playing merry hell on vacation and giving you a hard time?" John tried to hug her but Alice gently pushed him and said, "Ashwin's with your sister in Kerala and my sons are in London now. Come in Johnny, let me explain."

John could sense the lack of intimacy, affection and strange aloofness in Alice's voice. He also noticed for the first time her saying 'my sons' and 'Ashwin'. Somewhere at the back of his mind, he felt that once again his life had crumbled like a pack of cards.

John, then listened with grinding teeth, Alice narrating in a matter of fact tone, her hospitalization for cosmetic surgeries like 'mammoplasty' and'liposuction' to achieve her new dream figure., the news of divorce of Rini and her ex-husband and her repentant husband's reunion with their sons and his anxiety to join Alice.

"Ungrateful bitch, so you used me and my money to beautify yourself and acquire social skills which you could never have dreamed of. You were all along secretly preparing for this re-union with that bastard, while I was floating to provide money for all this. I'm sure you haven't forgotten your big, fat, ugly looks, your pathetic life-style with your two brats before I came into your life. I treated you with love and respect and gave you everything including my name and a-n-d ... look, what you have done to me. Oh! God! What a fool I was!" checking the uncontrollable urge to strangle the woman, who destroyed his life, John shouted.

Alice was extremely calm when she spoke, 'Please don't shout, I didn't fool you. Our marriage, let's face it, was a marriage of convenience. I did help to bring up your son; yes, I treated him like my own son, looked after your interests and was your loyal life, unlike your first wife who flirted around shamelessly. Well, I tried to improve my looks, acquired social skills, as you call it, but that was my right, yes, I earned it. What's wrong in accepting my repentant husband, father of my sons? Believe me, I'm grateful to you, but gratitude alone is not enough to hold on to a marriage. You of course loved Sajiv and Sujith; still you can't be their father, just the same as I can't be Ashwin's mother. We both are benefitted by our marriage, my sons had a father, your son, a mother for about 8years.Stretching our relationship further is disastrous, as Babu wants me back and my children miss me a lot. Please try to understand, let's part as friends." Alice sounded almost reasonable and convincing…

Captain John felt the urge to smoke which brought him back to the present reality. He lit a cigarette and inhaled it. Releasing the smoke in rings, he remembered how fate had brought Sarah to him quite unexpectedly.

It was during John's six months' stay in his widowed elder sister's house in Kerala, he met Sarah accidentally. Sarah, a middle school teacher was his sister's neighbor. John was introduced to her when she came to help his sister in making Ashwin's favorite 'rose cookies'. Later, from his sister John came to know that Sarah's father, a clerk in the Railways, had passed away leaving the burden of his family on the young shoulders of Sarah, two decades earlier.

Sarah had to give up her studies, to take up the job as a teacher. She educated her brother, saw him through his course in the Poly technic College, and married off her younger sister to the man of her choice. Years rolled by ,while Sarah was busy sacrificing her youth and life for her family .Of course, a pathetic tale but it did not strike particularly any sympathetic chord in John's soul, then. But, what triggered the whole affair was a chance remark from his sister.

"Poor Sarah, she was exploited thoroughly by her family. Her brother is in Kuwait with his family and her younger sister is well-settled in Bombay. They stopped even their annual visits to this place after their mother's death, a couple of years ago. Now they don't even visit or keep in touch with Sarah, how ungrateful! How can God punish such a good-hearted lady? She must've been very pretty in her hey days; now, she's in her mid-forties who would marry her? What a wasted life!"

A week after that conversation, John met Sarah on her way back from the church. It was a long walk and for the first time in his life, John talked naturally without any intention of making an impression on the listener. John noticed that though time had taken its toll, Sarah was still vaguely attractive with a strong determined face that silently spoke of her indomitable will to survive. When she smiled, she had the innocence of a child.

Somehow, the conversation took a different tone when Sarah spoke about her friendship with Ashwin. Without realizing it, John unfolded his strange, stranger-than-fiction, experiences to Sarah. When she listened, John could see her bright, expressive eyes flashing a variety of emotions, anger, pain, sympathy and sorrow…

That night John could not sleep a wink. Sarah's innocent smile, the tears she tried desperately to control while listening to his story, kept coming back to his mind. He knew it was not infatuation coupled with lust as in the case of Rini or sympathy masquerading as love in the case of Alice. This was a stronger, more mature and different emotion, a warm feeling and a tender affection for a woman, who had sacrificed her youthful dreams for her ungrateful siblings.

Moreover wasn't it destiny which brought another person exactly like him? Yes, a *persona non grata*, a person not wanted, not desired ,a nuisance to be thrown out of life, after using .After a sleepless night's tossing and turning on his bed, John decided to ask Sarah to share his life, to be his wife and Ashwin's mother.

The next morning, when John proposed to Sarah, she was not surprised. She was calm and a sort of serene look came to her, when she agreed to be his soul mate. Her only request was that the simple wedding should be in a church, as she firmly believed in the sanctity of marriage vows.

John was only too happy to be married in a church for the first time, though for his third marriage This time, of course it's "till death do us part", he almost muttered aloud....

HAPPY DEEVALLEY, I LOVE YOU, MA

Settled comfortably in the aisle seat of the aircraft, Lalitha looked around and noticed quite a few pattu sari-clad women with that usual 'frightened, first-time flyer' look on their faces, a common sight in flights to the US. No doubt, they must be the 'proud' mothers, flying to various parts of the US for attending their daughters' or daughters in laws' delivery, baby-sitting, cooking elaborate Indian dishes for the family craving to eat South Indian food etc. etc. After spending several months in the US soil, they came back to India wondering about the size of 'foot-ball' like egg plants, foot-long 'okras' and 'green cauliflower'(Broccoli was green cauliflower for many of the *mamis*) . She always pitied these women, often treated as 'persona non grata' by their children and had to return to India after months' of hard work, completely disillusioned and emotionally drained.

'Who am I to pity them? As though I'm going to have a great time. Poor Venkat, he gave me enough warning but, I was adamant to go to the US to see my son after a gap of three long years. Once, weren't we the envy of all parents, who had to wait many years to set their eyes on their NRI children, very often, till they fix their 'bride-viewing' and possible marriage? We were extremely lucky, Chintu was as good as his word visited India every year, right from his student days till he got married to 'that white girl', three years ago.............'

Lalitha switched on the movie channel to avoid the unpleasant thoughts but could not concentrate, as memories gushed through her tired brain....

Lalitha remembered vividly the day Chintu, their only son, had left for the US to do his Masters. That was the first time he was separated from his close-knit family. Trying hard to control her tears, she was preparing Chintu's favorite chicken, when he suddenly entered the kitchen and saw her in tears. Wiping her tears and hugging her close, he called "Appa, Sangeetha, come and see what ma is doing in the kitchen, she's crying her eyes out." Rushing to kitchen Venkat took over, "Lallu, why're you crying like this; we must be proud of him, right Sangeeta?"

"I don't understand, *Ma*, all these days you were bragging about Chintu's intelligence, talents and what not, now instead of encouraging him, getting emotional and making everyone unhappy", that was Sangeetha, their older daughter.

That was the time Lalitha voiced her worst fears, 'Once Chintu goes to the US, his coming back and settling in India is an impossibility, that's the magic of America; during his student days he can't come, later, job, green card and so many other issues. My heart breaks to think that he won't be with us for quite some time"

'Ma, I promise you that I would be in India every year even if it's for 10 days, Okay, after about 8 months, I'll be here, most probably for your birthday, just you wait and see' wiping her tears, Chintu said.

Chintu kept his words, he came to Chennai, forgoing even the money students usually make doing 'vacation' jobs. He brought a beautiful handbag, his birthday gift for his Ma, some electronic devices for his Appa's famous 'power –point' presentations in the University and makeup set for Sangeeta. All of them were ecstatic about Chintu's thoughtful gifts, till one day inadvertently he revealed the source of his income, the pittance he got for toiling at nights as a waiter in a Restaurant in the University Campus.

Lalitha remembered, how close she was to her son and how she could not make chicken or prawns, Chintu's favorite dishes, after his leaving for the US, till an enraged Sangeetha reminded her that she and her Appa too loved Chintu's favorite dishes and craved for home-made dishes...

Sangeetha's settling down in Bombay after her marriage was a real blow to Lalitha; she missed both her children, felt terribly lonely. Though Venkat also loved and missed his children, his extremely demanding job as a faculty in the Maritime University kept him too busy to miss them, like her....

One evening, when Lalitha was busy making a mental 'to do list' for Chintu's arrival in a week's time, that too, as an Engineer in a reputed company, Venkat came from his work and said excitedly, 'Lallu, I've great news for you, remember Captain Menon, and Prasanna Menon ,who visited our ship in Darling harbor, Sydney?' Menon joined my class for the, 'Refresher course for captains' today and.....''

Before he could finish, Lalitha interrupted "Oh, I remember them very well; they came with their beautiful daughter Swetha, who wanted to be a Doctor and remember we'......

Venkat said in an irritating tone, "Be patient Lallu, I'm talking about his daughter Swetha; she's doing her third year in Madras Medical College and also preparing for USMLE exams for going to the US. Menon wanted us to consider Swetha's marriage to Chintu and as she's only a student now, at least an engagement when Chintu comes next week, what do you say?"

"God is great, Venkat, He's answering all my prayers, just like Siddharth and Sangeetha, Swetha and Chintu too would make an ideal couple, I'm sure Chintu would be only happy, Swetha with her bubbling personality and charm would attract any young man; can't wait to break the news to Chintu, in any case we must insist on conducting the marriage in Guruvayur Temple." Lalitha whispered, raising her eyes towards ceiling……..

"Drinks, Ma'am?', the sweet voice of the airhostess and the noisy opening of bottles brought Lalitha back to the present .
Sipping her apple juice slowly, Lalitha deliberately brought her mind to the day, when Chintu confided in her the shattering news of Kerry, that 'white girl', as Venkat always referred her…

At first, Lalitha thought it was one of Chintu's usual bluffing even when he pulled the picture of a beautiful blonde with blue eyes from his wallet; Lalitha brushed it aside as a joke.

"C'mon Chintu, be serious, this must be some film star or model's picture, look Chintu, Swetha's   beautiful, talented and comes from a very respectable family, we've plans for a grand engagement in 'Taj'. Before we could invite Swetha for lunch, Appa wants me to find out about your convenience, that's all, no time for jokes now."

That was the time, with a serious expression, Chintu confided in his mother about Kerry, the details of her family, her trying to get a job near his work place, their decision to get married that June, as their combined savings was good enough to start a family etc...

Lalitha was aghast, she could not believe her ears, the young man sitting in front of her with definite plans of his future where his parents had absolutely no role to play, was her child, their only son......

The following week crawled by with Venkat trying to convince Chintu that the expected disaster of a marriage to a girl with totally different culture, and Chintu arguing that his Appa was quite unreasonable as he too loved and happily married ma, who belonged to a different caste and even State, against the wishes of his family, at the age of 25.

Later, at the airport ,when Chintu touched his Appa's feet while taking leave, Venkat with quivering lips, said, "All the best son, you're right, your Appa jumped a State and now you're jumping a Continent, Anyway, our blessings are always with you"

That was the last time Venkat spoke to his son.

But Chintu kept in touch with his ma through weekly phone calls, emails and even a picture of them, he in a fashionably embroidered Kurta, pajama and Kerry looking like Angelina jolly, in red silk sari.

Lalitha knew only too well that deep down, Venkat loved Chintu very much and his difficulty in coming to terms with Chintu's marriage was only because of the inevitable divorce, which would destroy him emotionally as well as financially.

Finally, after three years which seemed an eternity to Lalitha, she voiced her deep desire to visit Chintu just a couple of weeks before Diwali. And Venkat shocked her by making all arrangements for her perfectly timed flight to reach San Francisco on the eve of Diwali…..

At the Departure lounge of the Chennai Airport, Venkat held Lalitha's hands and in a voice choked with emotion said, "Lallu, I really doubt the wisdom of your going to Chintu's place, that too without me, I wonder how you would face the hostile reactions of that white girl, in any case be prepared, the moment you feel that you are not welcome, come back immediately instead of gulping down the insults, okay?" And   ignoring curious look of the onlookers, Venkat kissed her gently on the fore-head.

Wiping the tears at the thought of her loving, caring husband of thirty years, Lalitha sighed deeply.

'Ladies and gentlemen, this's Captain Smith…' The announcement of landing in San Francisco airport brought Lalitha back to the present. Clutching her handbag, Chintu's birthday gift for her and patting it gently to feel Chintu' favorite Diwali Sweets, her walk turned into a run, her anxious eyes searching for Chintu…….

Before Lalitha could realize, Chintu enveloped her in his bear-hug. Then, Kerry looking stunning in her simple outfit, a sleeveless light blue top and jeans handed her a huge bouquet of lovely roses and asked in a barely audible voice, her luminous blue eyes reflecting guilt, fear, anxiety and nervousness , 'May I…..I mean… can I …..hug you mom, no, no ma?'

Suddenly, Lalitha saw in Kerry, a confused young bride from Kerala trying to touch the feet of her Brahmin in-laws and their moving their feet off saying, 'not necessary', 'not necessary'………..

The next Lalitha remembered was her hugging Kerry closely and both of them weeping inconsolably…

During their two hours' drive home, both of them chatted like long-lost friends, exchanging the details of the family, job, their totally different culture etc. ,ignoring the comment of Chintu, 'What a chatter -box! Kerry can beat you hollow, ma!'

Next morning, Lalitha was woken up from her deep sleep by a red-silk sari-clad, stunningly beautiful blonde with a broad smile, greeting 'Happy *Deevallay* Ma'.
The lit *diyas* adorning their balcony wall, the marigold garlanded picture of Lord Krishna in the Pooja room and later, the grand finale, attending the Diwali celebration of Tamil Sangam, gave Lalitha the impression of their Diwali, back home …

On the way back from Diwali celebration, Lalitha could not help admiring Kerry's blue eyes, Kerry smiled and whispered in Lalitha's ear, "Well, well, don't know how to tell you, … Do you think, hmmm our child, I mean Chintu's and mine will look funny with Chintu's black hair and my blue eyes? You know Ma, my pregnancy test was positive".

Fiddling with her sari *pallu, Kerry* laughed, raised her sparkling blue eyes and looked at Lalitha .After a moment's hesitation, she asked,
"You want a grandson or granddaughter?" she laughed, her child-like innocent laughter………

That evening, Lalitha's chat to Venkat was a monologue narrating every single detail. Finally, Lalitha concluded, "So, she's not just 'that white girl', she's our daughter in law and…and she's going to make us grandparents this July and no excuses, you're coming with me to help our sweet, good-hearted daughter- in- law, Okay?"

Laughing away, Venkat said, "Lallu, put Chintu on, fast, let me congratulate him" ....